One, Wizard Place

Sidhe

BY

D.M. Paul

COVER ARTWORK AND INTERIOR

ILLUSTRATIONS BY

FRANK BERGER

This is a work of fiction. The events and characters described here are imaginary and are not intended to refer to specific places or living persons. The opinions expressed in this manuscript are solely the opinions of the author and do not represent the opinions or thoughts of the publisher. The author represents and warrants that s/he either owns or has the legal right to publish all material in this book. If you believe this to be incorrect, contact the publisher through its website at www.arcticwolfpublishing.com

Sentinel
All Rights Reserved
Copyright © 2006 D.M. Paul
Re-printed 2008 Arctic Wolf Publishing

This book may not be reproduced, transmitted, or stored in whole or in part by any means, including graphic, electronic, mechanical, photocopying, or recording without the express written consent of the publisher.
Arctic Wolf Publishing
http://www.arcticwolfpublishing.com

ISBN-10: 0-9817472-1-3
ISBN-13: 978-0-9817472-1-7

Arctic Wolf Publishing and the "AWP" logo are trademarks belonging to Arctic Wolf Publishing

Printed in the United States of America

This book is dedicated to my wife and daughter, for their faith and patience that these books might actually sell.

Thanks go once again to my editing wizard Deanna Brady. She can be found at getwords@getwords.net or getwords@gmail.com

Book 1 - One Wizard Place
Book 2 - Sentinel
Book 3 - Sidhe

Visit

www. onewizardplace.com

CONTENTS

ONE
Thieves in the Night

TWO
Bad Tidings Indeed

THREE
The Faerie Queen

FOUR
Kestrel

FIVE
Too Many Monsters

SIX
Poison Arrow

SEVEN
Yellow Eyes

CONTENTS

EIGHT
The Bog

NINE
Wailing Spirits

TEN
Watchers

ELEVEN
Faerie Dust in the Morning

TWELVE
Horror Stories

THIRTEEN
Tooth Faerie

FOURTEEN
A World Beneath

CONTENTS

FIFTEEN
Off to the Races

SIXTEEN
Upside-down

SEVENTEEN
The Bottom Line

EIGHTEEN
The Tree

EPILOGUE

Sidhe

-Chapter One-
Thieves in the Night

At night when the demons come...
sometimes they're real.

From the windowsill the little faerie demon listened intently as the old man snored in his sleep. The room was dark, and its eyes glowed a pale shade of green as it scanned the area for any sign that its task might be disturbed, but none was to be found. Silently it spread wide its translucent wings and leapt into the air, flying across the room and landing nimbly on the headboard of the bed, inches from the slumbering man.

The man mumbled something unintelligible, and the little demon went still. A few moments later the man rolled onto his side, and the twisted black lips of the faerie demon curled into a smile: the man had slipped into a deeper sleep. The opportunity was upon it, so it grasped the wooden headboard of the bed with its long, curved talons and lowered its head so that it was inches from the sleeping man's ear.

The demon was after information. The little beast's long, bare tail swished back and forth over the side of the bed as it whispered tales of doubt and fear, treachery and thievery into the man's unconscious mind. The man mumbled in his sleep but didn't wake as the demon weaved its magic into every word.

The sleeping archeologist was famous for his work with ancient Sídhe civilizations—those of the original fae, or Faerie, race—the first people. Unfortunately, many of the man's theories differed from mainstream academic concepts, and he had fallen from favor, becoming an outcast among his peers. For years he had tried to prove his presumptions but had yet to provide any hard evidence…until now. Recently he had discovered what he believed to be the original Faerie Tree—the one which had birthed the first of the fae people—and if the artifact that he'd brought back was really what he thought it to be, he would once and for all be proven right.

The faerie demon snarled when the man refused to give up his secrets. His mind was stronger than anticipated; but the demon had many skills and pressed its will into the magic.

The little beast played a hunch. *"The staff, what of the staff? It may be protected...but what if it is stolen? How will you reclaim the fame you once had?"*

The man rolled onto his back, not awake but clearly agitated by what he was hearing. He murmured something incomprehensible, then began to speak more clearly in his sleep.

"No, no...the staff is safely locked in the museum. Protected, yes...protected with the other treasures of the Sídhe. When the elves come, they will prove that I was right.... Tomorrow I'll show them."

The demon smiled. It had gotten what it had come for, but the timetable needed to be moved up. Tonight must be the night!

"Sleep well, old man, for I'm afraid you won't be quite so happy in the morning."

The nasty little creature leapt from the bed and

flew out the window. It dove downward through the congestion of the city and the streams of aerial traffic toward its rendezvous with the Sídhe agents who had accompanied it from the faerie realm on this task. It had retrieved the information they needed; soon they would allow it to return to the cool, dark forest where it belonged. No longer would it be forced to dwell within the stench of this foul city. Excited by the thought, it tucked its silvery wings into its sides and, weaving between the tall buildings, accelerated toward the ground.

When it reached the street level, it ducked into a dark alley and glided between the steel-and-concrete walls until it reached a seemingly abandoned warehouse at the end of a back street. The faerie demon landed on the edge of a rain gutter, its long talons clicking against the metal as it shuffled toward a broken-down ventilation fan. It slipped quickly between the blades and passed through the narrow duct, entering the building.

Within the old warehouse stood a miniature forest. It wasn't much in terms of acreage, but it gave

Sídhe

the Sídhe agents a small measure of home away from home. They were born of the forest, and they needed to be surrounded by clean air and woodlands to survive. The city, with all its noise and pollution, was simply too much for them, and the little glen provided a small respite from the urban environment as a center of operations for their search efforts.

The agents' keen Sídhe senses were alert to the small faerie demon's presence, although it made them feel uncomfortable. They despised the little beast inherently, for they felt it to be an abomination of their kind—a hybrid of an imp and a pixie. The Faerie Queen had bred this particular creature with the vile, insidious abilities of a demon but also the innate loyalty and obedience that all faerie creatures exhibited toward their monarch. She was determined that the creature would be an asset to her agents, and she insisted that it accompany them. Like the demon, they didn't have the inclination or strength of will to dispute their Queen, and as much as the agents despised this little monster of a step-cousin, they had to admit that it produced results.

The creature's magic was somewhat limited so

far away from its woodland home; even so, it had an uncanny ability to extract information from unsuspecting victims without their becoming aware of its presence. True to its devilish nature, it also enjoyed implanting unpleasant suggestions into the minds of those it tormented. This was the creature that whispered doubt and fear into people's dreams—the beast that kept them awake at night, fearing what the next day would hold.

The faerie demon weaved its way through the trees and landed on a low branch just out of reach of the three agents. It watched them for a moment, knowing full well how much they disliked its kind. It knew that turning over the information was the only way to end the quest and return home, so it smiled when they approached.

"The archaeologist has found the remains of the First Tree. The Queen was right; he has brought back proof of its existence. He has actually recovered the staff."

The three fae agents whispered amongst themselves, excited about what this meant. Their leader, a tall, lean, almost human-looking faerie with moss-colored hair, was the first to speak. The agent tried with difficulty to keep the sarcasm from his voice, for he knew the demon enjoyed toying with humans.

"What of the staff? Were you able to discern its location?"

The faerie demon's lips curled into a smirk. "Yes, I accomplished what was asked of me. And now, if you would be so kind and let me finish, I will tell you."

The lead agent suspended his inquisition and bowed ever so slightly to the diminutive creature. The faerie demon looked somewhat smug as it spoke.

"Currently the staff is located at the Cloudview Museum of Natural History. It's been locked away in the Sídhe exhibit with numerous other findings from the site. The exhibit is expected to open tomorrow for viewing. The archeologist anticipates that experts of various races and species will attend the gathering, but he is confident that the elves will be able to determine the authenticity of the relic."

The agents of the Faerie Nation looked

flustered; they hadn't expected this turn of events. They had been in search of the staff for so long that they never imagined it would be found by a human. If the elves proved the relic to be the true article, then its value would become immeasurable. The agents realized that the elves knew its true potential for power in the Faerie Queen's hands and would go to any length to prevent it from returning to her. It would be locked away somewhere and protected and might never be back in the possession of its rightful owners.

The leader glanced at his watch. "We still have time." He looked at his two companions. "Suit up! We have a job to do."

The half-breed demon watched as the fae agents prepared for the night's activities. The Queen had chosen them wisely and had prepared them with the necessary tools, skills, and training for such a task. Even on this short notice, they would be able to accomplish their mission.

The demon smiled. Soon it would be returning home.

Sídhe

Three silhouettes lurked in the shadows just outside the dim glow of the museum's exterior lighting. Only to the keenest observer would they have been noticed, as they wore fully camouflaging body-enhancement suits.

The Sídhe may have been forest-dwelling creatures that preferred nature and magic to science and technology, but the Faerie Queen recognized her people's shortcomings and adapted to compensate. Thus she had created a small cadre of subjects that specialized in advanced research and development in the area of defense, including weaponry and camouflage.

The three agents on this most critical of assignments were utilizing the latest advancements the department had to offer. The suits they wore were completely black and composed of exotic, naturally occurring polymers that absorbed visible, infrared, and ultraviolet light. This technology made them appear to the casual observer to be nothing more than shadows, invisible to heat-sensing devices that most security systems utilized. The technology also employed a full face-fitting helmet that enhanced their night vision, as well as a respiratory filter and communicator that purified the city's air and allowed them to communicate with each other without being overheard.

One of the agents removed a small device from a hard-sided utility pack he wore on his back. He aimed the instrument at the nearest streetlamp and pressed a small button. Without a sound the bulb burned out, and the side of the building was cast in shadow.

The lead agent nodded to the teammate with the device and removed a long, hollow pistol from his utility pack, along with a length of thin, black rope and a collapsible grappling hook. In less than a minute he had assembled the apparatus, unfolding the hook and attaching the rope to the end of its narrow shaft. He fished the line back through the hollow muzzle of the pistol and inserted the shaft of the grappling hook into the contraption. After one final check that the coast was clear, he aimed the gun toward the roof of the building and fired.

With only the slightest whoosh, the grappling hook exploded from the pistol, carrying the length of rope along with it and landing on the roof of the building. The fae leader then detached the pistol from the rope and placed it back in his pack. He tugged on the line and then, satisfied that it would hold, nimbly scaled the wall.

Moments later all three Sídhe agents stood on top of the museum building, with the rope pulled up behind them. Then the agents made their way across the roof to an enormous multi-paned skylight.

Structurally, the museum was designed like a giant corkscrew. A central ramp wound its way up from ground level, allowing visitors to view the exhibits as they climbed upward on a gradual slope. The main wings of the museum branched outward from the central ramp, with each major exhibit encompassing one entire loop of the large structure. The general design created a vast atrium within the center of the ramp, allowing daylight from above to filter downward, illuminating each of the floors.

It was still night. They stood at the edge of the vast skylight and peered down into the inky black depths of the museum.

"Adjust your helmets for infrared," said the lead agent.

His two companions obliged and adjusted the settings to view the proper wavelength. Quite to their delight, easy access to every level of the museum was possible with the use of just one rope.

The lead agent pointed to the spiraling ramp that encircled the circumference of the large complex and noted that every level was teeming with hundreds of semi-transparent red beams that crisscrossed every floor. Surprisingly, though, the central atrium below the skylight was free from any security devices.

The agent made a few adjustments to his helmet and seemed satisfied with the results. "It seems we have a few security measures to overcome," he told them, "but it looks like we only have to deal with the IR beams for the moment. I can't find anything directly below this window, though. Let's go in."

His partners nodded in response, without comment. Then two of the agents stepped back from the glass as the third removed the utility pack from his back and retrieved a metallic cylinder. He unscrewed the lid and poured the contents onto the closest windowpane.

In seconds the gooey, green substance began to react with the glass and dissolve away its surface. Moments later a gaping hole formed in the skylight, easily large enough for the agents to slip through. The lead agent took hold of the rope they had used to scale the side of the building and attached it to an anchor point on the roof. He lowered the rope through the hole, being careful not to let it reach the ground floor, where it might trip some unseen pressure sensor.

The lead agent held the rope and stepped to the edge of the hole. "I believe the Sídhe exhibit is on the seventh floor," he told the others. "See you down there!"

Satisfied by all the green indicators on his heads-up display that his suit's counter-measures were active, the agent grabbed hold of the rope and lowered himself through the opening. He repelled downward to just above the seventh floor and gauged the distance to the closest railing. Through the enhanced vision of the suit's display, he saw that the security beams zigzagged across the room, right up to the edge of the balcony railing, but did not include the railing itself. Pleased, the nimble fae agent swung his rope back and forth until it put him just over the handrail. With one final swing, he stepped onto the narrow ledge and balanced himself just out of reach of the closest security beams.

Less than two minutes later all three agents were balanced on the handrail of the seventh level of the museum. The lead agent gazed around the room, finally focusing on a sign on the opposite side of the open atrium. With his gloved hand, he pointed to the new exhibit.

"We need to get to the other side of this level. If what the little demon said is true, it should be located over there with the other findings."

His two partners nodded in agreement, and they made their way around the cavernous room, balanced precariously on the narrow handrail. When they reached the exhibit, they spotted numerous display cases containing various artifacts that they recognized as remnants from long-forgotten times. The centerpiece of the new exhibit was a tall glass case that held only one item, and even though they had never seen it before, they immediately recognized what it was. This was the culmination of eons of searching. At long last, one of the Great Staves would return home to its rightful owner.

The lead agent flipped a protected switch within his suit, and a red indicator appeared on his heads-up display. To the naked eye, nothing had happened, but through the enhanced technology of the agents' vision systems, they could see that their black suits had turned red.

The agent at the rear of the group removed a small sensor from a side pocket on his utility pack and studied the electronic readout for a moment. "The suits exactly match the spectrum and wavelength of the infrared beams crisscrossing this level. We should be safe for the time being, but don't dawdle too long—the power drain on them is enormous."

Without another word they leapt from the railing and headed across the room in the direction of the artifacts. They navigated their way through the beams of light, confident that their new suit technology would allow them to pass through the security measures, and allow the beams to pass around them without breaking the infrared signal.

When they reached the case, all suit indicators were still in the green, and nothing had alerted them to an alarm being set off, either silent or audible. Careful not to cross any beams with an item not protected by a suit, the second agent removed his utility pack and withdrew a metallic container similar to the one used earlier on the skylight. With a syringe, he withdrew a portion of the gooey, green substance and traced a thin line around the edges of the glass case. A long section of the glass melted away, and with the third agent's help they were able to pull it away and set it to the side without tripping any security measures.

The second agent reached into the case to remove the staff but stopped an instant before he touched the ancient artifact. "Wait!" he told the others. "I'm not picking up any security countermeasures, but I don't have a good feeling about this. Check the pedestal for something that we might be missing."

The third agent nodded and removed a small

laser scalpel from his pack and burned away the case's metallic lower pedestal. Sure enough, he found an archaic-but-effective tripwire attached to the base of the staff where it was mounted in the case. If the second agent had removed the staff, he would have disturbed the tripwire and set off an alarm.

A moment later the wire was defused, and the staff was free from its bonds. The second agent removed a long, black sleeve from his pack and slid the staff into it. He connected the sleeve to his suit with a small wire and then synchronized the two items. Then he pressed a button on the sleeve, and the sheathing glowed red, exactly like his suit.

With the connection to the suit, he noticed that his already diminished power supply suddenly began to drain away rapidly. "We have to go. The sleeve's power supply must be shorted—it's draining my suit. I don't have much time!"

The lead agent nodded, and they all sprinted for the railing, but the agent with the staff had taken only a few steps before his infrared countermeasure flickered and died away altogether. A moment later a siren went off, and the lights in the museum flashed on. A second after that, a massive cage dropped from the ceiling, separating the other two agents from the one with the staff.

The highly experienced agent was far too skilled to give up so easily. He yanked loose the connection between the sleeve and his suit, and at the same time he hurled the staff to the lead agent before it could become trapped with him inside the narrow bars of the cage.

The lead agent caught the staff, still within the useless sleeve, and hesitated for only a moment. He looked back at his trapped compatriot. "Get out if you can," he called out, "but if you cannot…you know what you must do."

The trapped agent nodded in return without speaking. He watched as the lead agent and the third team member raced to the opposite side of the atrium, where they could make their escape. The last thing he saw of them was the rope being pulled up through the skylight so that they might buy themselves an extra few seconds to get away.

-Chapter Two-
Bad Tidings Indeed

Commander Devin Crashblade stood at the edge of the Sídhe exhibit, just beyond the border of red tape that indicated it was a crime scene. Tall and muscular, his black hair shot with silver at the temples, he was quite a distinguished-looking figure, with a career to match. He watched as his team scurried efficiently around the scene, looking for bits of evidence that might provide a clue to who had been behind this museum robbery. The theft had taken place hours before, and they had been on the scene since early morning, but nothing of any consequence directly related to the crime had been found.

Normally Crashblade would leave the investigating to his agents, but something seemed fishy about this case. He was concerned that it could go unsolved if they didn't come up with something soon. Although the investigation was nearly wrapped up, he still wanted to do some probing for himself.

The last few technicians packed up their gear and carried it away from the scene. Crashblade waited until they were all out of sight before he began to remove the barrier of red tape so that the exhibit could officially be reopened to the public. He was disheartened to learn that they hadn't discovered anything of any real value. Other than a hole in the skylight far above and a dismantled display-case alarm trigger, the investigation had come up relatively dry. He'd had an electronic inventory of the museum run earlier in the day, and the only object missing had been the artifact from this exhibit; other than that, nothing else seemed out of place.

The case just didn't add up. The museum was full of priceless antiquities, but all that was stolen was an ancient, albeit unusual, staff. There was definitely more to this case than met the eye.

The officer was just removing the last of the tape when the museum's curator approached.

"Well, Commander? Did your agents discover anything…any leads?"

The commander looked down at his feet and shook his head, trying to piece together what to say. Devin Crashblade was one of the finest leaders the Incantation Enforcement Agency had seen in years. His success rate since the agency had been under his command had far outweighed any of his relatively insignificant failures. To say the least, he wasn't used to issuing this kind of news. Frustrated, he pointed his finger at the broken skylight and repeated what little he knew.

"Unfortunately I don't have much to report. We have located what we believe is the entrance and egress point of the robbery's perpetrators, but beyond that we found little else to go on, at least initially. Technicians have taken samples of the skylight and the display case, as the glass seems to have been dissolved rather than broken through. If we can determine what substance was used to accomplish that, we might have a better idea how to track down another lead or two. The problem is that this kind of testing takes time, and the artifact might be long gone by then. I've put the highest priority on the lab tests, but even with expedited results, I'm afraid we could be too late."

The curator nodded, troubled by the possibility; but since he knew Crashblade's reputation, he realized that the commander must certainly be taking whatever actions he could to prevent that happening.

"I see," he replied. "I'm sure you and your agents are doing everything possible to get to the bottom of this."

Just then a commotion at the end of the corridor caught both men's attention. An elderly man with long white hair was running right toward them. A string of IEA agents were right on his tail, but he barely managed to stay a few steps ahead of them.

Noticing that the curator remained unruffled, the commander put his hand on his weapon but didn't remove it from its holster as the elderly man raced up to the curator and grabbed his arm. The IEA agents hurried to pull him away, but the curator spoke up to calm everyone.

"It's all right, Commander…I know this man.

He's an old friend and is the source of this exhibit. He, of all people, stands to lose the most from this unfortunate event."

Crashblade nodded to the curator and gestured to his agents. "I'll take care of things here," he advised them. "Just finish packing the gear and get back to headquarters." Then he turned his attention back to the two men. *Might as well let the old man speak,* he thought. *Maybe he has something useful to add.*

The elderly man released the curator's arm and looked at him for a moment. "What happened here? I heard that the museum was robbed."

The curator patted him on the back. "Don't worry too much…only the staff was taken. Nothing else was touched."

The elderly man's head fell and his shoulders drooped, but he seemed resigned to the situation. "I just knew the staff wouldn't be safe. I've been worried about it all day."

The older man looked at the commander, seeming to only just realize that he was standing there. "The staff is everything…it's the proof I've been searching for, for so long! They'll never believe me now." He shook his head in disgust and drifted into the exhibit.

The commander waited until he was out of earshot before speaking again. "So, what was that all about?"

The curator watched the elderly gentleman wander among the artifacts. "He's the archeologist who found all these ancient treasures. Many years ago, in his youth, he was famous...quite a prodigy in his field. He specialized in the Sídhe people and their mysterious history. Along the way his theories shifted and strayed from mainstream ideals."

The curator slumped slightly and then went on. "He became obsessed with his new ideas and fell from grace, an outcast from the archeological community. He's spent a lifetime and nearly all his family fortune trying to prove his theories true. We had for the most part given up on him, but recently things have changed."

The curator hesitated slightly as the man came back into view, waiting to continue until he was out of earshot again. "Tonight is his night to shine. He's somehow found proof of what he has been harping on for these years. I gave him a chance and allowed his findings and these artifacts to be authenticated by experts from around the city—even an elf from Greylok is coming to the opening of the exhibit. The centerpiece was to be the staff. If what he thinks is true, the staff is the final piece to the puzzle and is physical proof of his outlandish theories."

Crashblade nodded, taking everything in. "So, if what the archaeologist says is true, and these artifacts are indeed what he thinks they are, a lot of his peers stand to lose a good bit of their dignity tonight."

The curator hadn't thought about it that way before but nodded in agreement. "Yes, that's true. Quite a few of us will look like fools. I suppose most of us stand to lose a measure of respect if he was actually right all along."

Suspects. Crashblade watched the old archaeologist wander through the exhibit, then looked at the curator again. "Sir, if you don't mind, I think I'll stick around for a little while. When do you expect the experts to arrive?"

The curator almost grinned. "I don't mind at all if you stay. The others should be here any moment, and after what you just pointed out, it seems that even I could be considered a suspect."

Commander Crashblade smirked ever so slightly at the way the curator had seemed to read his mind, but he refrained from any comment.

A few minutes later, a small group made its way up the ramp toward the new Sídhe exhibit. The commander turned to watch them as they entered, counting five in all, but saw no sign of an elf. He was looking for something out of the ordinary, hoping that one of these individuals might give something away, but they seemed oblivious to his scrutiny. They were far more intent on making it into the exhibit.

Cloudview is a vast city made up of countless races and cultures, so it didn't come as a shock to the commander when he realized that not one of the group was human. They oozed, padded, crawled, and slithered into the exhibit, all heading straight for the artifacts. Crashblade was extremely experienced in his field, and he watched each of them as they wandered around, scrutinizing the items. They all clearly kept their distance from the old archeologist, but after what the curator had said, that didn't come as any surprise to him.

The commander's instincts were honed to a razor's edge, but none of the individuals gave him a bad feeling. All the experts seemed focused on the ancient artifacts…more interested in the science than in what might become of their reputations. They didn't seem to have had any part in the crime, but Crashblade felt that a little more probing might be warranted.

The commander stepped into the exhibit area and listened intently to the conversations going on all around him. He was wearing a Merlin Z language translation device in his ear and had little trouble understanding the various dialects. To be certain not to miss anything, he pressed a small button on his watch and began to record a few of the conversations, just in case his normally sharp instincts were a little duller than usual.

The commander's gut feeling was that no one in

attendance had anything to do with the robbery. He watched the elderly archeologist for a few minutes and followed him around as he conversed with a few of his peers, but even he seemed devoid of any foul intent.

Crashblade was focused so tightly on the individuals in the room before him that he hardly noticed anything else until a hand landed on his shoulder. He spun around and found an old friend smiling back at him.

"Enob, what brings you here?" Crashblade asked the tall, slender elf. Then he remembered that an elf was supposed to be among the experts invited to authenticate the findings. "I have to say that it makes me a bit nervous that the High Wizard of the Kingdom of Greylok is the expert who is representing the elf nation." The commander shook his head back and forth and laughed to himself. "I had a funny feeling about this robbery, and your presence doesn't make me feel any better."

Enob smiled and clasped the commanders hands. "It's good to see you, too, my friend."

They had been friends for too many years to

Sidhe

count, but every time Enob showed up in the city, trouble seemed to be right behind him. It had been less than a year since their last encounter, and the old wizard looked the same as ever. Unfortunately, their last meeting wasn't something either one of them would soon forget, and the commander was sure it had left him with a few more gray hairs.

On his last visit, the wizard had brought with him the bad tidings that one of the greatest warriors of the elves had been possessed by the dark soul of a black dragon. If they didn't stop that dragon, the wizard had explained, he would recover an ancient artifact that would bestow upon him nearly limitless powers. Fortunately, with the help of the warrior's young apprentice and two agents from the Incantation Enforcement Agency, Enob had been able to overcome nearly insurmountable odds and thwart what could have been a disaster of global proportions.

Crashblade watched as Enob pulled back the hood of his purple cloak, exposing his long, flowing white hair, and made his way to the Sídhe artifacts. The display cases had been opened by the curator, and the experts were free to examine as they saw fit, so long as they didn't damage any of the items in the process. The elf moved about the exhibit with ease, occasionally scrutinizing a specific object more thoroughly than the others. A short, well-crafted dagger caught his attention, and he examined it for a long while, particularly the ancient runes inscribed on it. The elf wizard then removed a dusty text from his pack and compared the markings on the blade with images in the book. For a long while he studied the little weapon, performing all sorts of strange tests, both magical and physical, with the aid of advanced technological devices he had brought along with him. After a while he nodded to himself and turned his attention to the old archeologist and smiled.

"You've done well."

The elderly man's eyes flared and his frown ebbed. It seemed a weight had been lifted from his shoulders.

Enob called over the other members of the group and gathered them together in a small circle. The wizard allowed the scientists to argue amongst themselves for a few minutes before taking control of the gathering.

"I believe we all have an apology to make to this man," said Enob as he gestured to the elderly archeologist. "Unless anyone here has scientific justification to prove otherwise, I am convinced that these artifacts are proof of his claim that the First Tree existed and that these relics are pure Sídhe."

Enob held up the dagger for all to see. "The workmanship and markings on this weapon are clearly of Sídhe origins. I see no trace that its design was influenced by any of the other races. Through both technological and magical means, I can deduce that this item was crafted during the age in which the First Tree was thought to have existed. The markings on this blade are pure, and from what I have gleaned from the most ancient of texts, I can only agree that it originated during the first civilization of the Faerie race, from the original Sídhe people."

The group of scientists mumbled and argued for several minutes, but in the end they could not object. The data simply didn't lie. These items were truly ancient—more than just very, very old—and the markings could only have originated in the ancient faerie realm. Over the years bit and pieces of evidence surfaced that alluded to the myth of the First Tree, but never had it been proven that the Tree truly existed. The implications were staggering: from this Tree the first race of the world was born, and all of the others evolved from them. The elves in particular were an early offshoot of the Faerie race, and they were only the first of countless races to have developed from the true Sídhe stock.

Enob held still for a moment to let them finish grumbling. "Ultimately the staff would have been the final piece to this puzzle. It was said to have been carved from the Tree itself. Even without the staff, however, I believe we have enough evidence to re-evaluate our theories and continue the science that this man began formulating so long ago."

Enob left the scientists to argue amongst themselves, but he knew that only their arrogance could stand in the way of the truth. Everything was laid bare tonight, and he knew they would eventually give in to their scientific natures. Countless years of work lay ahead of them, but at least tonight one man was vindicated for holding true to his beliefs despite many years of ridicule and prejudice.

Commander Crashblade followed his old friend over to the damaged display case where the staff had resided only a day before. The wizard closed his eyes and ran his hand across the empty case, murmuring to himself in a strange, magical tongue. When he had finished, he nodded his head in approval and stepped up to a waist-high pedestal next to the case. Crashblade depressed a small button on the pedestal, and a projector in the ceiling glowed for an instant before coming to life. A cone of light shone down directly over the base in front of the two old friends and displayed a perfect holographic image of the staff.

Crashblade said, "We had copies of this image made and have distributed them around the city in the hope that someone might recognize the staff before it disappears into a private collection."

Enob nodded but didn't comment. He wandered around the three-dimensional image, studying it from every angle. The staff was tall, approximately six feet in length, and had been carved from a single piece of gnarled gray wood, with veins of silver swirled and streaked along the length of it. For the most part, it was unadorned, except for a series of mystical sigils and runic characters that had been carved into the wood along its length. In addition, three intricately carved leaves protruded from the finely fashioned head of the staff in what appeared to be the same silver material that ran through the grain of the bark.

Enob shivered at the ramifications of what he had apparently deduced from this examination. He touched the commander on his shoulder and looked him the eye. "Let's talk in private."

Crashblade nodded, noting fear in the elf's expression and his voice. *Great!* he thought. *Here we go again.*

The two of them walked away from the damaged case, but something quickly stopped the wizard in his tracks. He looked at the floor for a moment and stepped backwards, and a slight smirk appeared on his lips but was gone again a moment later.

Sídhe

He moved forward toward the outer ramp and rested his back against the balcony railing, away from anyone else who might be listening. He then looked toward the Sídhe exhibit for a moment, trying to gather his thoughts. Finally he spoke again.

"I assume that you are somewhat familiar with the myth surrounding the existence of the First Tree."

Crashblade nodded. "When I heard about this case, I refreshed my childhood memories."

Enob smiled. "What the myth doesn't mention is very important, and I tell this to you only because you are familiar with the history of the Wyrd." He was referring to an ancient stone tablet with a single word inscribed upon it. This word, once spoken, gave the speaker nearly limitless power.

"What I said earlier to the group is true," he continued. "The findings here come from what I believe is the First Tree. As I'm sure you recall, when the Builders created this world, they used the Wyrd to create the First Tree, and from that tree the fae people—the Sídhe or Faerie race—were born. Later the Sídhe created two staves from parts of that tree—one from the very highest of branches, reaching far into the heavens, and the second from the deepest of roots, pulled from the very bowels of this world."

Crashblade nodded, and Enob continued to recount the history of his earliest ancestors.

"The tree stood for countless millennia, but eventually it simply outgrew the limits of its physical form and couldn't support its own weight. It fell to the ground and broke apart, dropping seeds in its wake. In the eons that followed, these tiny seedlings spread and became what we know as the Great Forest."

Crashblade listened with focused attention, as it was rare to hear this tale directly from a descendant of those Old People who was himself a powerful wizard. Although the commander had heard and read the general story more than once in the past, he knew that Enob could communicate details that would not be available from another source.

The elf went on. "When the Tree fell to the ground, the hearts of the fae people fell with it. Without a home they began to argue amongst themselves, and eventually this conflict escalated until civil war broke out. There was no clear victor in that now-forgotten war, but the outcome was obvious: the Faerie Nation broke apart like the Tree. The Sídhe ancestors scattered across the world and, over time, adapted to their new environments, evolving into the various races that exist today.

"A few of the original Faerie people stayed behind in the rubble of the Tree. They nurtured the newly fallen seedlings and became the first of the elves. My people most closely resemble the original fae folk, as we sprang from what is considered the purest of their bloodlines...the ones that remained behind.

"An even smaller number of the royal Faerie bloodline never left the fallen Tree. They stayed with it while the other races began to evolve and move on. Some small measure of magic was retained in its shattered husk, protecting them from any evolutionary changes, and their blood remained pure. Over time, even that measure of magic began to fade as the Tree rotted into the earth. Eventually they were forced to leave their ancestral home and seek refuge in another location.

"Eons passed, and the new city of Cloudview began to be constructed. The remaining pure Sídhe found their way to this new home and, using a powerful, ancient form of magic, they created a world for themselves on the thirteenth level of this city. There they have remained in self-exile, isolated from the outside world. They are ruled by the Faerie Queen, a distant descendent of the original inhabitants but also a direct descendant of the royal Faerie bloodline.

"It is said that both of the staves from the Tree were lost during the time of their civil war. For every Sídhe ruler since that time, one task has remained paramount…and that has been to recover the staves. From one generation to the next, each monarch has hunted tirelessly for the most sacred of Faerie artifacts, but until recently neither staff was ever found.

"The staff you see here in this projection is what I believe to be one of the two lost relics. If my assessment is correct, this particular one was crafted from the tallest branch of the Tree, and it is potentially the more dangerous of the two. This was the prouder of the two talismans, and within it resides immense potential power. The Faerie Queen is fair and honorable in her own right, but she has little control over her genetic makeup. Once the staff is in her possession, she will be at the mercy of its latent energy."

Commander Crashblade looked down at his feet for the second time that day, wishing he had taken up a different occupation. "Do you have any idea of what the staff can do?"

Enob shook his head from side to side. "I have some vague guesses but nothing substantial. I can say this, though: I doubt it will be good for any of us."

-Chapter Three-

The Faerie Queen

Commander Crashblade took a step back, shifting his weight from one foot to the other. "How can you be sure the Faerie Queen was behind this robbery?"

Enob looked away from the commander and glanced back toward the Sídhe exhibit to determine if anyone had been listening or watching the two of them. Satisfied that no one had, he pushed himself off the railing and walked back into the exhibit with the commander at his heels. The wizard took a few steps into the room and paced back and forth for several moments, gazing at the floor and muttering to himself. Then he focused his attention on a particular spot on the marble flooring and removed a piece of white chalk from a hidden pocket within his long traveling robes.

Using the chalk, he drew a large, unbroken

circle on the smooth marble and traced a series of magical figures around the edge of the ring. He uttered several incomprehensible phrases and wove his hands through the air above the strange markings. The circle and the symbols began to glow a pale green and flared brightly for a brief second before dying out completely. When the glow had diminished, a small mound of sparkling silver dust could be seen near the center of the circle.

Enob bent down and ran his fingers through the silver powder, pinching a bit of the strange substance between his thumb and forefinger. He looked up at his old friend and smiled wanly. "Faerie dust…. I'd say one of them didn't make it out of here alive."

Crashblade studied the glistening powder for a moment and looked up at the ceiling. "When we arrived early this morning, the containment fence had been dropped, separating the exhibit from the ramp. We had to have it lifted before we could investigate the crime scene, but we couldn't find any evidence that anyone was trapped behind the gate."

Enob shot him a wry grin. "No one left in this

world, at least...."

The two remaining Sídhe agents stood on a bluff overlooking the vast landscape of the Park. The green space on the thirteenth level of the multi-tiered city of Cloudview was certainly big, but *big* wasn't really the right word for it. Neither were *huge, enormous,* or *gigantic*.... None of these words could describe the Park accurately.

The city of Cloudview as a whole was actually many cities stacked one on top of the other, with the largest and tallest of each city's buildings supporting the next level. Generally speaking, this basic design allowed for access to any of the sub-cities from any of the open sides of the massive tower that was Cloudview, but the Park was different. It wasn't enough to build a city-sized park—not nearly enough. From the beginning the designers wanted the Park to be very special, and a tremendous amount of effort was put into the magic behind its construction.

First of all, unlike the rest of the city levels, the Park had only one entrance. This single access point was actually a quantum-dimensional compressor. Once inside this special entrance, beings and objects were shrunk down to one thousandth of their normal size. From the outside, the Park had the same physical dimensions as any of the other sub-cities that made up Cloudview, but inside the sealed complex, everything was actually a fraction of what its size would be, or used to be, in the outside world.

To be inside the Park was like being on a separate continent. Traveling from one side of the complex to the other literally took weeks, as it was thousands of scale-miles from end to end. In order to take advantage of the enormous space that was created inside the Park, it was terra-formed to resemble the outside world. Vast mountain ranges, lakes, swamps, open plains, inland waterways, enormous stretches of untamed forest land, and even an ocean teaming with sea life were constructed in an exact likeness of the real thing. Rocks, trees, sand—everything was identical to its larger, real-world counterparts, only physically much smaller in size.

From the beginning it was decided that the Park

would remain untamed. It was populated with a wide range of creatures from around the outside world and was to remain a relatively uncharted wilderness. Only a few civilized races took refuge in the vast expanse of wild territory. The Faerie Nation occupied a massive old-growth forest near the center of the complex, and a small community of sylvan elves guarded the deep woodlands, a few days' journey from the main entrance.

The remainder of the immense terrain was inhabited by the numerous wild creatures of the world. Occasionally a small number of the more organized tribes of warlike races vied for dominance, but in general the Park was loosely under the shared control of the countless creatures that lived within its magical walls.

The remaining two Sídhe agents stood on a rocky outcropping overlooking the rugged landscape of the Park. Using a magical whistle, they called for transportation back to their homeland; but after waiting for more than an hour they started to worry. Without any form of proper transport, it would take them weeks to reach the safety of their forest on foot. To have accomplished so much only to fail this close to the completion of their task would be devastating.

They had been in the city for nearly a year, tracking down one lead after another and ultimately running into one dead end after another. After countless red herrings, they had caught a real break and, through their network of sources, learned of an archeologist and his recent discovery. They worked that lead, and in the end they hit pay-dirt, but getting to that point hadn't been easy. The work was difficult and was made more so because they were determined to remain hidden from the rest of the populace.

For the most part, they had escaped through the city with relative ease, but their fear of pursuit weighed heavily on them. It would only be a matter of time before the investigation of the robbery would lead to them. The fae agents did not underestimate the intelligence behind the Incantation Enforcement Agency, and they knew full well that they had left far too many clues behind.

Of course this was never the intention, but they

couldn't have known that their timetable would escalate so quickly, and they weren't able to cover their tracks nearly as well as they'd wished. When the demon had provided them the latest intelligence, they knew it would be necessary to move immediately and were forced to react. Their intention was to recover the staff and cover up any tracks that might lead an investigation back to the Faerie nation, but because everything had happened so quickly, they were forced to leave behind a warehouse full of evidence and, what was much more important and quite tragic, one of their own.

As a race, the true Sídhe were very rare. For countless generations they had remained isolated within the protective walls of the Park, rarely venturing into the city or the outside world. Their mere presence outside their homeland would only have generated suspicion, so they opted to remain hidden, working solely with what information they could glean from their network of spies. When they needed to probe deeper, they utilized the faerie demon. Its size allowed it to slip between the buildings and homes with great stealth, and its talents granted them access to information when they needed it extracted.

Only on the rarest of occasions did the agents themselves venture out, and when they did they concealed themselves in various cloaks and cowls to hide their true appearance. For the most part, it wasn't so difficult to remain undiscovered—physically they were of about the same height and physical proportions as the elves that frequented urban environments far more often—but without a disguise they could be distinguished from their close cousins rather easily. Unlike elves, their skin varied in shade from a pale green to a gray-brown, and although they wore their hair long, as did the elves, it had a distinctly leafy texture and ranged in color from a mossy green to a deep red-brown, usually streaked with silver.

Now the two remaining agents were back in the Park but not yet in their homeland. When their dracon-fly steeds finally arrived and landed on the bluff where they were waiting, both agents let out an audible sigh of relief. They wanted nothing more than to get as much distance between themselves and the entrance to the park as they could. Only when the staff was in their

Queen's hands would they truly be able to relax.

Their mounts had been waiting for them for nearly a year, but time meant very little to the flying beasts. These creatures were hybrids of sorts, a cross between a green dragon and the four-winged insects that bore a similar name to their own. In fact they were far more dragon than insect, and the only real similarity they bore to their insect cousins was in the wings. Unlike a typical flying reptile, a dracon-fly had four membranous wings and a smaller, more streamlined body than that of a true dragon.

Three of them landed on the bluff, one for each of the agents on the original team. They eyed their masters with a curious look. They were intelligent creatures, bred to bear the faerie folk safely over the dangerous lands that they called their home. With their pale, glowing eyes, they could see that something was wrong, and they clawed the ground with their long, black talons. Each of them had waited for its master's return, patiently hunting the lands far from the dark forest that they were accustomed to inhabiting.

The lead agent approached the largest of the

three beasts cautiously, letting the animal smell his exposed open palms with its long reptilian snout. Satisfied, the creature bent low and allowed the team leader to stroke it along a thin, nearly translucent crest that began just behind its eyes.

The Sídhe agent turned to the smallest dracon-fly of the three and bowed his head low in respect for his fallen ally. "I'm afraid your master won't be returning with us, but his sacrifice has not gone unrewarded. After eons of searching, we are once again in possession of one of our nation's most sacred relics."

The agent removed the long staff from its protective bag, holding it out for the creature to see. The intelligent dracon-fly at once recognized the staff for what it was, but that did little to alleviate her feelings of grief. Like most of her kind, she was deeply attached to her master, and she roared in protest.

The lead agent returned the staff to its protective covering and stroked the creature's long, sinuous neck. "You are free of your debt to our people; no longer must you carry us upon your back. If you wish you may return with us to our homeland or be free of us altogether—it is your choice."

The dracon-fly looked at the agent, and a long moment of silence passed between the two of them. Then the loyal creature straightened out her long neck and roared at the sky, her pale green eyes glowing with an internal fire that burned in the afternoon light.

The steed didn't move from the rocky bluff but waited for the agent to make the next move. She had made up her mind. The Faerie people had treated her kind well for eons, and the mutual pact between them had worked nicely. She would seek a new master when they returned to the Sídhe realm, and together they would continue the work that her previous master had begun. Until that time she was determined to finish this job, and she would stay with the team until the staff was returned to its rightful owner.

Without words the agent understood what the dracon was thinking and responded to her. "Good," he said. "We can certainly use your skills to keep us from trouble on the long road home."

He looked over to his partner, and they moved back against the rocky wall of the bluff. The lead agent touched the wall and ran the palm of his hand across the rough surface. When he had found the exact spot, he traced a magical symbol on the rock wall and then pressed on the rune as it glowed dimly in response.

A portion of the wall was compressed inward, revealing a small cave where the taskforce had hidden their riding gear and traveling clothes. They were relieved to find a thin layer of dust coating the equipment, indicating that nothing had been touched in their absence. Satisfied, the two agents removed three saddles and various stores they would need for the trip home. There was no point in leaving behind any further evidence of their passing, so they opted to equip the third dracon with all of her previous master's riding gear and supplies.

Once the dracon-flies had been saddled, the two agents removed their city attire and donned their riding gear. Happy to be free of the clothing that still bore the stench of the city, they packed everything away into their saddle bags and secured the staff where it would be safest. After a final check that everything was in place, the two agents mounted their flying steeds and made themselves comfortable in the leather saddles.

Situated between the two pairs of wings of his mount, the lead agent slipped his booted foot into the stirrups and pressed his heels into the dracon-fly's flanks. He looked back at his teammate and nodded, urging the creature forward at the same time. The dracon mewled in response and raced forward, leaping off the cliff face and diving down towards the seemingly endless stretch of forest far below them. The creature accelerated downward, keeping its four wings tucked into its sides and allowing the drop to continue unhindered. Hardly twenty feet above the trees, the dracon-fly lifted its head to the clouds and spread wide its four wings, allowing their thin, membranous material to catch the wind and arrest the fall.

The other two dracon-flies followed their companion's lead and leveled off a few yards behind. Then, using the currents of warm air that flowed upward from below the forest canopy to keep them aloft, they skimmed above the treetops, nearly invisible to any aerial predators that might be looking for an on-wing meal. The fae agents needed no instrumentation to guide them home. They could feel the call of their Queen, and they settled onto a heading that would take them back to her with as little interruption as possible.

The Faerie Queen had sensed the exact moment her agents had touched the ancient staff, and her blood surged in eager anticipation of holding it, herself. After so many Faerie rulers before her had failed, she would be successful. Finally countless eons of searching had paid off, and one of the sacred staves would be back where it belonged—in the hands of the Queen of the Sídhe.

Already the magic of the staff called to her, filling her with power and determination; but as the spell began to take hold, a dread that she had never before experienced overwhelmed her. She shuddered as outlandish thoughts raced through her mind, but she was helpless to resist the magic. Even at a distance she couldn't oppose the magic, and a cold shiver ran down her spine. Now preparations needed to be made for its arrival.

The faerie hound at her feet lifted its great,

silvery, deer-like head off its paws and looked up at its mistress. Keenly aware of her every emotion, it sensed her anxiety and stood up with a long stretch. It peered at the Queen with its electric-blue eyes and nuzzled her thigh.

The Queen reached down from her throne and patted the magnificent creature, scratching behind its silky ears. "Shhhh...there, there," she murmured. "I know you feel my pain, but there is little I can do to resist. Soon the staff will be here, with its rightful owner, and I will be at the mercy of its full power. Already it has asked more of me than I am willing to do, but even now I can't defend against its pull, although I fear that this alone will upset the balance of our world and beyond it."

The Faerie Queen was almost unbearably exquisite, in a way that only the fae races could achieve. Her skin was a delicate, almost imperceptible pale shade of mint, and without blemish. Her features were as fine as the most talented sculptor could fashion only in his wildest imagination. Her eyes were the color of the sea before a storm, deep gray-green pools that seemed to burn with an inner fire. Highlighted with reds and yellows, her bark-colored hair fell in a wave to the middle of her back, and she emitted the perfume of flowers blooming in the springtime. Truly she was beauty embodied in near perfection.

"Come, my friend. I have a difficult task to accomplish, and I need you at my side for support."

She rose from the living tree that served as her throne and threw aside the blanket that protected her legs from the cold marble floor, thinking, *What it will ask of me when it is in my hands, I can only imagine.* With the faerie hound at her side, she padded away from the throne. As they walked, she stroked the hound's neck, causing the animal's long, silvery barbs to lift upward slightly.

Somewhat resembling large greyhounds, most faerie hounds stood slightly more than three feet tall at their well-muscled shoulders and usually weighed more than two hundred pounds. Magnificent, silvery coats of dense fur protected them from the elements and from any stray claws or teeth that might slip through their other defenses. They had vivid blue eyes that radiated intelligence, and cunning senses kept them alert to their surroundings at all times. For defense they had strong jaws filled with a mouthful of razor-sharp teeth, and their long, slender, powerful legs terminated in deadly sharp claws.

The most unusual feature of the faerie dog was a crest of barbs that extended from just behind the creature's ears, with the longest barb beginning behind the neck. The hardened quills lay flat and ran in single file down its spine, finally tapering off at mid-back. When the dog was in defensive mode, however, the barbs rose up and spread outward from its back

The faerie hound looked up at its mistress with its impossibly blue eyes and growled softly, keeping perfectly in step with her every move. They were alone in the throne room and unhindered by the usual escort of guards or servants. Earlier she had dismissed them for the night, her intuition telling her that she would need to be alone this evening. They had left reluctantly, comforted only by the knowledge that her hound would be with her.

Since the time of the First Tree, faerie hounds

had been guardians over every generation of the royal bloodline. Totally loyal to their charges, few creatures could provide protection as well as they.

The Queen and her canine companion traversed the empty halls of her upper chambers until they reached one of the castle's outermost walls. She pulled back an ornate tapestry hanging there and, starting from the floor, ran her slender fingers along the mortar of the stone, tracing the shape of a narrow door. Once she had finished the outline, she pressed her open palm onto the center of the wall and pushed inward. The invisible line she had drawn burned yellow for a moment and faded away as the stone wall swung inward on silent hinges, revealing a secret passageway in the wall.

A cool rush of wind greeted the monarch and her canine protector as they stepped into the opening. A narrow tunnel ushered them to a spiraling staircase that wound its way upward in a steep ascent. Unhindered, they climbed the stairs until they reached a small wooden door that was bolted shut. The queen released the bolt, and they stepped out the door into the night.

They stood on the tallest of the castle's spires in

a spot that offered them a perfect panoramic view of the surrounding forest. For a moment the Queen admired the beauty and solitude of her realm…which she knew was all about to change.

She knew what had to be done, and she strengthened her resolve in preparation for the onset of the magic. Raising her arms into the air, she began to hum softly. Her body trembled as the magic welled within her diminutive figure until she was shuddering from the exertion. Her pupils dilated and expanded outward until they encompassed her eyes entirely in pools of burning silver.

She pressed her will into the magic of the spell and allowed it to drift upward into the air, where it was picked up by the wind and carried out over her kingdom and into the surrounding countryside. For many long moments she held the spell together, giving the magic time to saturate the land, until finally she could bear it no longer. The Queen slumped to the cold stone floor of the castle's parapet. The fire in her eyes faded, and she allowed herself to give in to exhaustion.

Her last conscious sight was that of her faerie

Sidhe

hound, huddling next to her so that it might protect her from the cold.

-Chapter Four-

Kestrel

Kestrel Greenleaf held tightly to her saddle as her squirrel steed clung to the underside of a branch in one of the many giant trees of the Park. Gently she prodded the furry creature in the side, and it leaped silently from the branch and attached itself to the massive trunk of the tree. At this height, the elf scout was still having difficulty spying on the three hobgoblins she had been tracking for the last hour, and she decided to move a little closer.

The finely crafted mesh armor of both the rider and her squirrel mount made hardly a whisper as the animal inched down the trunk on clawed feet. A gentle pull on the leather reins from Kestrel stopped the squirrel in its tracks as it was suspended vertically on the tree, waiting for its next command. They were still more than a hundred feet from the ground, but that was as close as the elf dared get for the time being.

With her keen elf vision, she focused on the hobgoblins. As expected, her movement hadn't been detected by the evil brutes on the ground below. She knew exactly what they were up to, but she waited and watched patiently, hoping that it wouldn't be necessary to intervene.

To the well-trained eyes of the scout, it was apparent that the foul beasts and their Thraken hunting dogs were stalking a previously wounded griffon that was trying desperately to elude the persistent hunters. Kestrel had spotted the creature a few minutes earlier and knew right away that it was quickly losing ground to the scavenging hobgoblins. One of its wings had been torn savagely, and it was bleeding from numerous other wounds. She looked up into the tree canopy and wondered what had forced the griffon from the sky. Judging from the raggedly torn wing and the long slashes along its leonine back, a dragon had likely brought it down; but without the marauder in sight, it was hard to say for sure.

The hobgoblins had probably spotted the aerial

fight from the ground and, thinking this would be an easy catch, taken up chase. Fully aware that a griffon's feathers and pelt would bring them a fortune back in their village, they surely couldn't miss the opportunity. Why the dragon—or whatever creature had driven the formidable griffon from the sky—hadn't claimed its victory wasn't clear, but whatever the case, the creature had been grievously wounded. Now it was only a matter of time before the hunters caught up with it.

Foul, stinking beasts, the hobgoblins were one of the few organized tribes that inhabit the wilds of the Park. Cousins to the goblins, but with a more aggressive streak than their smaller relatives, they waged a never-ending battle to gain a higher standing in the food chain of the untamed lands. The hairy humanoids stood more than six feet tall and weigh about 300 lbs. They had feral eyes, pointed ears, and small, boar-like tusks that protruded from their lower lip. Aggressive fighters, they armored themselves in leather and crudely crafted chain mail. Most preferred long hunting axes for close combat but really weren't overly particular about the weapons they used. They had brought along with them Thraken hunting dogs, which they had cruelly bound to long iron chains attached to spiked collars around their necks.

Evil by nature, these dogs had little fear of other creatures. They had short, rough, brown coats with patches of black and red markings, and when agitated, their eyes glowed cherry red. They were clever trackers, known to relentlessly hunt down and corner their prey. Typically hunting in packs, they were renowned for their stamina and the ability to block potential escape routes. For these reasons they had become the favored instruments of the hobgoblins.

Kestrel cautiously watched the hobgoblins from her perch high in the tree. Two of the creatures had hunting dogs with them, and she wondered why the third did not. The elf looked more carefully at the group and noticed that the third hobgoblin was dragging behind it a long, rusted chain, but she didn't hear the telltale whines and whistles of another hunting dog.

Her curiosity didn't last long. When she heard a rustling of leaves a short distance away, the hairs on the back of her neck stood on end. She slammed her heels into the sides of her squirrel, wrenching the creature around the trunk of the tree. A moment later an emaciated grimalkin leapt from a nearby branch and latched onto the trunk where the squirrel had been a moment before. It had blue-black fur and a body that seemed to be nothing more than muscle and bone. The savage and stealthy carnivore ground its long claws into the bark of the tree and glared at the elf with fiery orange eyes.

Kestrel wasn't interested in lingering there, and she whirled the squirrel around while continuing to press her heels into its sides. The grimalkin slashed out with its claws and raked them across the hind leg of the squirrel as it turned. Fortunately the leather wrapping of the light elven armor held fast, and no real harm came to her mount, although the long gashes in the leather sizzled from acid released by the creature's claws.

Terrified, the squirrel raced farther up the tree and leapt onto the first branch it could find, while Kestrel held on for dear life, attempting to regain control of her runaway steed. The grimalkin growled and followed right behind. Trying to gain as much distance as possible on the pursuing creature , the squirrel sped blindly down the tree limb until it bent low under their weight. An instant before the branch gave way, the frightened squirrel sprang away and leapt to the next branch, grabbing hold precariously and clawing its way on top of it.

Kestrel looked back and spotted the grimalkin racing after them. It lashed out again and again, slashing the air with it claws, but the squirrel managed to stay one step ahead. Leaping from one branch to the next, the squirrel remained just out of reach of the fierce cat's deadly grasp, but the beast was unrelenting and wouldn't let them go.

The elf scout knew that her panicked squirrel couldn't keep up this pace much longer without making an error that would send them both to the ground far below. A desperate plan came to her and, without thinking about the consequences of a possible mistake, she put it into motion.

Kestrel unbuckled her safety harness from the saddle and abruptly pulled hard on the reins, forcing the squirrel from the branch. The creature sprang off the limb in a twisting descent and fell onto another branch nearly twenty feet below. Just as the squirrel grasped the limb with all of its claws, Kestrel threw herself from the squirrel's back and grabbed hold of the branch, as well.

As she hoped, this sudden maneuver bought them an extra moment, and the seasoned elf scout pulled herself to her feet and yanked her sword from its sheath. Blinded by its own fury, the grimalkin didn't notice the elf and continued barreling toward the squirrel. It soared through the air directly toward Kestrel, realizing too late that a trap had been set.

Kestrel braced herself for the impact and at the last moment slashed upward with her sword, slicing the foul creature's belly with the elven blade. The beast smacked into the branch and clawed at the bark to grab hold, but its balance was lost, and it fell away into open space. Kestrel watched as it fell. They were more than a hundred feet off the ground, and she knew that it had no chance of surviving a fall from that height. As an elf, and especially as a ranger, she abhorred violence; but in her role as a scout, deep in the wilds of the Park, it was often necessary for survival.

Her distaste for killing the creature lasted only a moment, though, as she spotted the three hobgoblins still roaming the forest below, searching for the wounded griffon. She had a job to do, and that was to stop them before they could find and kill the magnificent creature.

Even nimbler than most of her kind, Kestrel raced quickly across the tree branch in search of her squirrel. It was a well-trained creature, and she knew that it wouldn't go far once it realized the grimalkin was longer in pursuit. When she reached the massive trunk, she stopped and whistled for the animal. The squirrel heeded her call and raced obediently up the tree to rendezvous with her. Kestrel climbed back into the saddle and pointed the creature toward the ground. Although it was unlikely that the hobgoblins were still unaware of her presence, it was time to face them head on.

A moment before the squirrel leapt to the ground, one of the hobgoblins burst out of the scrub, oblivious to her approach. Instantly it spotted the grimalkin on the ground and howled in fury. It wanted nothing more than to kill whomever had done this. Kestrel knew its anger wasn't for love of the fallen beast. Grimalkins were very costly and not easily trained. From the looks of its emaciated stomach and the scars around its neck, this one had been mistreated horribly; the hobgoblin must have starved and beaten the creature into submission. She knew that its anger stemmed from that fact that it would have to find another of the rare creatures and abuse it repeatedly until it also obeyed its cruel master.

Less than a second later, the hobgoblin spotted Kestrel atop her squirrel and in a very vulnerable position...or so it thought. It lifted its ax over its head and rushed towards the elf girl. With blinding speed, Kestrel had a great ash bow in hand and an arrow nocked before the monster had taken two steps forward. Oblivious to the danger, the hobgoblin ignored the threat and pushed forward. Kestrel fired the bow, and with a *thwack* the powerful arrow tore through the armor of the beast and into its chest.

Propelled forward by rage and ignoring the

pain, the monster continued to rush them. Too close for another shot, Kestrel released her harness and vaulted off the squirrel, throwing herself at the creature. The hobgoblin swung the ax, but the angle was wrong, and it managed only to brush by her shoulder as she slammed into the creature's chest.

The hobgoblin was big—far bigger than the diminutive elf—but the force of the impact was enough to stop its forward progress, knocking it backward slightly. With her arms still outstretched, Kestrel pressed in against the massive chest of the monster until she could smell its fetid breath. By shifting her weight and using the creature's backward momentum, she flung herself upwards and somersaulted over the confused monster's head, landing in a crouch behind it.

The hobgoblin stopped dead in its tracks and dropped its ax to the ground. Then it looked down as it felt a warm rush of liquid under its filthy armor. It reached its hand to its chest and found the handle of a dagger that had been slipped between the armor and plunged into its heart. A moment later its eyes rolled back in its head, and it fell to the ground.

Kestrel glanced around for the other two hobgoblins while she prodded the beast with the toe of her boot. Satisfied it had been dispatched, she reached down to retrieve her long dagger, methodically wiping the blood from its blade on the grass and returning it to its sheath.

The elf ranger leapt onto the back of her squirrel, and they bounded off in the direction of the wounded griffon. She wasn't sure where other two hobgoblins had gone, but she hoped she would reach the creature before they could. Kestrel and her squirrel weaved between the trees, searching for fresh tracks on the ground. Finally the elf spotted a faint trail through the low-lying foliage of the forest floor, and her mount followed it until they found a small clearing surrounded by the giant trees.

The griffon sensed her coming and dropped into a defensive posture. It was a beautiful and intelligent creature, with the head, forelegs, and wings of a giant golden eagle and the body of a muscular lion. Kestrel knew immediately that it was weak from its wounds and was very afraid. She also knew well enough that there was nothing more dangerous than a scared, wounded creature, especially one who thought it was cornered.

Elves are far more attuned to the world around them than many other beings. They have an innate sense of the feelings and emotions of the wild creatures that inhabit the land, but Kestrel's abilities in this regard seemed to exceed even that of her kin. On some subconscious level, she could make a deeper connection with other creatures and communicate on the most primal levels.

Ignoring the danger, she dismounted her squirrel and approached the wounded griffon with caution. She moved slowly toward the animal with her palms open. Immediately she made a mental connection with the intelligent creature and created a kind of empathic link between them. The griffon allowed her to approach, and she stroked the side of its head to comfort it.

The connection broke when a horrifying whine distracted their attention, and they both tensed at the sound. The Thraken hounds had caught the scent of the griffon and were getting closer.

The hobgoblins smirked when they entered the clearing but continued to hold fast to the chains of their hunting dogs. The beasts whined and growled, straining their necks against their bindings and drawing blood with the torturous collars. Pleased, the hobgoblins held tight to the dogs, allowing their blood lust to overwhelm them.

By then Kestrel had her bow in her hands and an arrow nocked. The thought of killing again made her stomach turn, but she knew it would be necessary to save the griffon and herself. Instinctively she knew that the world would be a better place with a few less of the demon-spawned predators, but it still bothered her deeply to have no choice in the matter.

The tension in the air was palatable. Kestrel knew that if she didn't fire first and kill at least one of the dogs before the hobgoblins released them, she would have four creatures to fight at one time. Nonetheless, her personal code of conduct stayed her hand; she couldn't bring herself to kill without one of them making the first move.

Sidhe

The lust for a kill burned in the dogs' eyes. The hobgoblins couldn't contain them for much longer, and slowly they drew in the chains and began to release the clasps. Before the beasts had a chance to attack, something in the air changed, and the dogs calmed down. A cold breeze blew through the clearing, and goose-bumps rose on the backs of Kestrel's arms. There was magic carried on the wind, and the elf scout could feel it take shape all around her. A beautiful voice called to her, begging her to come; but the elf easily shook off the strange enchantment, resisting the call, and the voice died away with the wind.

The weak-minded hobgoblins weren't so lucky. They turned in place, confused and entranced. For a second they couldn't figure out what to do; then the magic took hold and had them completely enthralled. Moments later they gave up on the griffon and wandered back in the direction from which they had come. Even the dogs had been overcome by the call and provided no resistance to their chains, allowing their masters to lead them out of the clearing.

Kestrel slid her long ash bow back over her

shoulder and returned the arrow to its quiver. She reestablished the link to the griffon's mind and listened to its thoughts. Apparently it had also heard the call but had just as easily resisted the magic as she.

Not expecting a response she spoke to the magnificent creature. "What do you suppose that was all about?"

Exhausted, the griffon lay down in the soft grass of the clearing and allowed Kestrel to approach it. She pulled her pack from her back and dropped it to the ground, digging through her supplies until she had what she wanted.

The elf removed a water bottle, a clean cloth, and a small, unmarked jar. She unscrewed the lid carefully and allowed the griffon to smell what the jar contained. "This is an old recipe given to me by my grandmother," said the elf, smiling. "I can't tell you what's in here, because it's a secret, but it'll fix you right up."

Her spirits were high. A moment before she was nearly forced to kill; now, because of some strange series of events, she didn't have to, and she could help the wounded griffon without interference. The experienced elf scout knew that this wasn't some bizarre trick of the hobgoblins—they'd clearly had her outnumbered, and frankly they didn't have it in them to trick her. The magic had simply overcome them, and all of her instincts told her that they were really just gone.

She reached out with her awareness, but oddly enough the whole area seemed clear of predators... no danger at all... which in itself was a very weird situation. This kind of thing didn't normally happen in the Park—it was a dangerous place—but she trusted her own keen senses. They had kept her alive in this unforgiving land for many years, and there was no reason to lose faith in them now.

Kestrel turned her attention back to the griffon. "This might sting a bit, but I promise it won't hurt for long. I need to clean and treat your wounds so they don't become infected."

She could feel the griffon's agitation, but she knew that it trusted her. She dampened the cloth with water and wiped the dirt and dried blood from in and around the gashes on the creature's back and sides. The griffon flinched every time she cleansed the wounded areas, but as soon as the healing balm was applied, the great beast seemed to relax.

It took nearly half of an hour before she had all the wounds cleaned and treated, but when she was done, she was satisfied that the griffon would be all right. The wounds were deep, and if left untreated they would most likely have become mortal. She knew that if she hadn't come along, surely this creature would have died.

For another hour she allowed the griffon to rest, keeping watch over it as it began to heal. There were still no predators about—the forest was quiet, *oddly* quiet—but she figured that this couldn't last after dark. There were only a few hours left until sunset, and she knew they would have to find a safe place to sleep.

She stroked the eagle-like beak and looked the creature in the eye. "We need to get you out of harm's way. Even a creature like you isn't safe out here in the open. I know this area well enough; I'm fairly certain I can find a nice cave where you can rest and heal. How about if you follow me, and I'll show you?"

Sidhe

The griffon understood and stood up. The young elf was surprised by the solid connection she had made with the creature, but she wasn't about to argue the point. A whistle brought her squirrel out of the forest, but after one look at the griffon, it kept well behind the two of them.

Less than an hour later, the three companions arrived at a shallow cave set on the side of rocky bluff. After making a cursory inspection of the cavern for occupants, the elf scout led the griffon inside. It was small and cramped, but Kestrel thought it would provide shelter and protection from both the elements and any unwanted visitors. Luckily a fast-running stream was nearby, and she knew the creature would be able to hunt and fish with relative ease until its strength returned.

With the griffon safely tucked away and its wounds treated, the elf scout turned her attention back to the hobgoblins. What kind of magic had so easily taken control of them?

That wasn't just any magic, she realized. *That was what fae folk called* the glamour—*the power to enchant the mind!*

She thought back to the sound of the voice—a woman's voice—and she knew immediately who it was. *Only one creature commands that kind of magic, but why would she do such a thing? Why would she want to control such monsters?* There was only one way to find any answers to these questions, and she knew what she had to do.

-Chapter Five-
Too Many Monsters

Kestrel waited for the griffon to fall asleep before she allowed herself to close her eyes. She needed a bit of rest before heading back into the wilds, and an hour or so of quiet would rejuvenate her strength and help her sort through the events of the day. She had trouble falling asleep, though, and couldn't get the enthralling magic out of her head.

Why would the Faerie Queen have called such vile monsters to her side? The only way to get to the bottom of this would be to follow the beasts to wherever they were headed, but she was already overdue back at her own village. By the time she could travel home and return, however, the trail would be cold, and she might never learn the reason the hobgoblins had wandered off.

All this just didn't make any sense, and she knew that her curiosity would get the better of her. In the end she decided that there was no point in fighting the matter. With her mind firmly made up, she made herself comfortable next to the griffon and allowed sleep to overcome her. In a few minutes she slipped off into dreamland, satisfied in the course that lay ahead.

Hours later the young elf scout woke with a start. The cave was dark, and it took her a moment to reorient herself, but the loud snoring of the griffon brought everything back in an instant. She glanced at the creature and hesitated, fearing for the sleeping animal's safety and wondering if she was doing the right thing, but one good look at the powerful animal reminded her that few predators would dare disturb this beast while it rested.

As if on cue, the sleeping creature rolled to its side, stretched out one of its massive claws, and barely missed slicing her in half in the process. There was nothing to worry about—anything brainless enough to venture into the cave would most likely become an easy snack. The worries for the griffon's safety set aside, she turned her attention back to the matter at hand. It was time to track down the hobgoblins.

Less than an hour later, mounted on the back of her squirrel, she picked up their trail. They had made no attempt to conceal their tracks, and the fast-moving squirrel quickly made up for lost time.

Kestrel had little trouble following the trail. Her keen vision allowed her to see the infrared spectrum of light. Even on the darkest of nights, she could discern the movement of living creatures from the heat signatures left by their footfalls. Her elf eyes gave her the capability of shifting subtle variations of heat into complex images, and she could see nearly as well in the dark as she could during the day.

The tracks were cool, and following the waning heat residue left by the hobgoblins was difficult, but she managed to pick her way through the dense underbrush of the forest floor, guiding her squirrel in the direction they had gone. She discerned from the color of the footprints that they were many hours ahead of her, but it didn't really matter. She wasn't looking for a fight, just an explanation as to what was going on. As long as she could follow the trail, she would eventually catch up to them.

An hour or so later, the elf scout sensed a slight variation in the night sky and determined that daylight was less than an hour away. When the sun rose, she would have to switch back to normal vision, and she would lose the telltale heat signature left by the hobgoblins. In the light of day, tracking the beasts might prove slightly more challenging, but she was an expert tracker and doubted this trail would be too difficult to find.

The day after the investigation at the museum had concluded, Enob bade his farewell to Commander Crashblade and returned to the elf kingdom of Greylock. Only in his vast library could he better understand what the Faerie Queen would do with the staff once it was in her hands. He had some notion as to the power it held, but he wasn't sure of what that meant.

Crashblade had provided the wise old wizard with a holographic representation of the staff, and he studied the image for a long while, trying to understand more about the magical device. The ancient runes and symbols etched on it intrigued him the most but were beyond even his vast knowledge. For hours he poured over his mystical tomes, trying to decipher their meaning, but the strange language was so old that it predated his impressive collection of resource material.

The wizard spent the entire day and most of the evening trying to make sense of the fae writing. Finally exhausted, he collapsed on his desk, his head stuck in one of the many open books scattered across the room.

That night he dreamed of dragons. Somehow his subconscious mind had picked up on a tiny detail he had overlooked during his long search though the many books.

He woke a couple of hours later, not exactly refreshed, but excited that he might actually have dreamt the answer. He pressed the switch on the holographic projector, and the image of the staff materialized in front of him. One of the symbols did look familiar—slightly different from what he was used to seeing, but still recognizable.

The wizard pulled from his shelf a dusty old

book of dragons and flipped through the yellowed pages. Almost immediately he came across the symbol he was looking for, and it nearly matched the character carved on the staff. It resembled a dragon.

Fear welled up inside the old wizard. *Could this staff call the dragons?* But what use for controlling the formidable beasts would the Sídhe have? He seriously doubted that, even with the magic of the staff coursing through her veins, the Faerie Queen would consider using the beasts to go to war for her. *To what end? What would that bring her and her kingdom?*

Setting aside that unlikely train of thought, he turned his attention back to the book so as to understand better the meaning of the symbol. To his surprise the answer was actually right in front of him. What he'd thought was a long-forgotten representation of a dragon—any dragon, for that matter—was actually more specific in nature. He flipped the pages from one to the next and realized that nearly the same sign appeared on each of the pages but differed slightly from one to the next.

From his readings he learned that the symbol

depicted more than just a generic dragon: the slight variations in the shape of the figure actually specified its particular color. A few pages later, and he came across the exact symbol that was etched on the staff. In the book the sign was the mark of the green dragon, and Enob soon realized that the symbol carved on the staff did not refer to a dragon after all, but rather simply to the color green.

Like so many other signs, its original meaning had evolved into a more complex connotation. It had most probably started out as simple symbol for the color green, but because of its strange shape it came to represent the dragon. By changing the design slightly, the character could be used to specify any particular color of the beast.

With new light shed on the marks carved into the staff, Enob was able to discern many more of the ancient sigils. It would take him days to fully decipher the context of the entire staff precisely, but a general understanding of their meaning became clear to him. He found the symbols for air, sun, earth, and water. Superficially these were just depictions of the various elements of the world, but together they meant more than that. His final discovery was what he believed to be the symbol for life or, more importantly, growth. Then a novel theory popped into the wise man's head, and he looked at the staff anew.

For a long moment he studied the carved head of the staff, and in particular the circular carving there that was surrounded by finely crafted leaves. He suddenly became aware that he'd been so intrigued by the complexity of the runes that he hadn't realized it, but the answer had been staring him in the face all along. The head of the staff was fashioned in the shape of an acorn. Air, earth, water, and sunlight: these were the most basic elements, the essential ingredients for life, but they were also the simplest of instructions.

The staff housed a seed, and the Faerie Queen would use her most powerful magic to plant it.

A full day and a half after the battle with the hobgoblins, Kestrel was still tracking the foul beasts. Enthralled by the faerie glamour, they were making excellent time—nearly running, from the look of their tracks—and only stopping to rest for short periods.

As she closed in on their trail, it became easier to follow, but she wasn't in any particular hurry to overrun them. Keeping a good distance behind them provided a measure of protection in case they weren't as enthralled as they seemed. She needed to find out where they were going and report whatever information she could glean. From their general direction, they seemed to be heading straight for Myrr Wood and the Faerie kingdom. Of course that would make sense if it were the Faerie Queen who summoned them, but secretly she hoped that maybe it was a mistake.

With only a few hours of daylight left, the trail became complicated. At first only a few set of other tracks were mixed in with those of the hobgoblins, but shortly thereafter hundreds or maybe even thousands of tracks cut in from every direction. A twenty-foot-wide tract of vegetation had been trampled in a broad swath of destruction that looked like an army had plowed through the vicinity.

The elf scout began to feel very uneasy about the whole pursuit. She dismounted from her squirrel and wrapped herself in her camouflage cloak, proceeding on foot so as to approach unheard and hopefully unseen.

Nearly invisible, she slipped undetected into the undergrowth beside the newly cut trail, so quiet and well concealed that she could have passed unnoticed by a creature standing only a few feet away. Confident that her soft elvin boots weren't leaving a trail on the fallen leaves of the forest floor, she paralleled the newly cut trail and followed it for a short distance.

The crunching of leaves stopped her in her tracks, and she dropped to her belly in the light brush. Two hulking orcs suddenly stepped from the vegetation on the opposite side of the trail and then began following it.

For several excruciating moments, Kestrel held her breath as the foul-smelling beasts walked right past her. The large humanoids with gray skin, lupine ears, and pig-like faces had long, snaggled teeth that jutted from under their lips. From their size and copious braided facial hair, Kestrel recognized both these orcs

Sidhe

as males. Orcs had a longstanding hatred of elves, and the young scout wasn't interested in a confronting these two. They were apparently decent fighters, with far too many notches in their well-used weapons.

She waited until they had long since passed by before she stood and continued her parallel course beside the beaten trail. With her keen hearing, she picked up on a commotion further along the trail and moved deeper into the surrounding woods. As she got closer to the sound, she was forced to drop down again to her knees and watch as more than twenty orcs pushed through the foliage on either side of the trail and regrouped in the middle of the path. All of them were as well armed as the first two she had seen, and each carried a large pack overflowing with supplies and weapons.

The lush forest canopy overhead was beginning to thin, and the elf scout knew she was getting closer to the edge of the forest. A few minutes later, she came to the border of the woods and found herself atop a steep cliff that dropped about two hundred feet to the valley floor below. The sheer cliff wall below her was nearly vertical and very difficult to climb, with only a narrow trail that switched back and forth from the cliff down the wall to the floor below. Between the rock face and the forest lay a short expanse of open grassland intermixed with a few boulders that had broken away from the cliff wall. Just beyond the grassland, stretching as far as the eye could see, lay the vast Myrr Wood and the kingdom of the Sídhe.

Generally speaking, the trees in the Park were huge—easily large enough for the elves to use horse-size squirrels to navigate the upper canopy on an intricate highway of branches that linked each tree to the next. The trees were also very old, as old as the Park itself, and were direct descendants of the behemoth trees that formed the Great Forest in the world outside Cloudview. The largest of the trees in the Park exceeded a thousand feet, with trunks hundreds of feet around. Still, compared to the trees of the Great Forest, they were mere saplings.

When the Sídhe had established the Park eons ago, they had taken seedlings from the Great Forest and planted them from one end to the other across the wide terrain. For their own kingdom, though, they had taken their magic a step further. The few times the young elf scout had looked upon the immense stretch of old-growth woodland, she was both amazed and terrified at the same time. The trees of Myrr Wood were big, hundreds of feet tall, but with twisted, gnarled trunks of black bark that were strangled with ivy and moss. In contrast to the dark, foreboding trunks, the upper canopy of the forest was a beautiful green—impossibly verdant—a shade of the color that should not by rights be attainable in the living world.

Never had Kestrel been in the depths of the dark woods, in the eternal gloom where only an occasional narrow beam of sunlight slipped through the dense leaves to drive away the shadows. The trees there were different from other trees, for they had nearly evolved into sentient beings, and to those who traveled within their realm, it seemed they were constantly being watch by thousands of unseen eyes. It was not a place for unwelcome guests.

On this day it wasn't the woods that drew Kestrel's attention, but rather the surrounding grassland

One Wizard Place

that separated the woodlands from the cliff. Spread out across the edge of the forest were hundreds, possibly thousands of vile, menacing creatures. An army of monsters had begun to form what appeared to be a defensive ring about the dark woods. Hobgoblins, orcs, bugbears, trolls, goblins, ogres, and even gnolls formed the bulk of the evil gathering. Normally mortal enemies of one another, they had all somehow been brought together to share a common goal. This was strong magic, indeed, for under any other circumstances the area would be the scene of a gruesome battle, with the dying bodies of these blood enemies scattered across the grasslands.

The creatures had gathered into groups of fifty or more each, and Kestrel watched in amazement as they prepared their defenses and built encampments for what appeared to be an extended stay. Many of them had brought along their favorite fighting animals and chained them at the perimeter of their defenses for added protection. Thraken hunting dogs, great, muscular Scarpothian ridgebacks, demon-jackals, massive cats such as the grimalkins, and the most deadly of them all—the nawg—lay in wait at the ends of thick iron restraints.

As Kestrel watched, more and more fiends joined the ranks, swelling the numbers beyond anything the young elf scout had ever seen or imagined. Understanding the magnitude of the information she had just gathered, she knew that she needed to return immediately to her kin and report this ominous news.

Just as she was about to slip away, the world went silent. The quiet was so deep that Kestrel could hear the thumping of her own heart, and it seemed that all the forest stopped to listen. Then the light of the world dimmed, and the sky went black for an instant.

Neither had this happened in her life nor had she ever even heard of such a thing. She was aware that she was in the Park on the thirteenth level of the great city of Cloudview and understood that the sky above her was only a magical representation of the outside world: although thoroughly real in appearance, it was merely an illusion, albeit on a massive scale. Still, the magnitude of the event was utterly unsettling.

The blackout lasted only a few seconds, and the

sky quickly returned to normal. It was if a tremendous energy spike or surge had collapsed the city's power grid, and it took the huge generators a moment to catch up.

A dim green glow appeared near the horizon—too far away to pinpoint exactly, but originating somewhere near the middle of the deep woods in front of her. It intensified and grew in size until it spanned the horizon from one end to the other in a great emerald ball. With it came a rush of wind, a wave of pressure that ripped leaves from the trees and knocked her onto her back. As soon as the windstorm had passed her by, the glow on the horizon diminished and shrank back beyond her line of sight until it disappeared altogether. She needed no confirmation that whatever had just happened was somehow tied to the dangerous army surrounding the Sídhe realm…and that the Faerie Queen was surely the source.

Kestrel was so caught up in the moment that she didn't hear the scuffling sounds behind her, and she realized her mistake too late. She was more than two hundred feet above the grasslands, with no possibility of her presence being detected by the not-yet-watchful eyes of the gathering army, but when she heard the noise, she cursed herself for not examining the encampments more closely. If she had she would have realized that more than a few of the restraining chains were not currently restraining anything.

The elf scout's scent had been picked up by the sensitive nose of a demon-jackal. It howled, and Kestrel tensed instantly, realizing she had been found and that the call would bring more unwanted company. She bolted away from her place of concealment to try to gain as much distance from the creature as she could, but already its call had elicited the help of two of the dreaded nawg.

In an instant the chase was on, and the nimble elf darted through the woods, leaping over logs and crashing through the thick vegetation. When she hit a stream that she had crossed over earlier, she dared to look back and realized that her pursuers were only a few seconds behind. She bounded from one boulder to the next, dearly hoping she wouldn't slip into the water and sprain an ankle. Once safely across, she dove back into the woods in hopes of buying some time in the thicker tangle of trees, but then she heard splashing and knew that the hunters hadn't lost her trail for even a second.

The situation had gotten worse, and she heard the indecipherable ranting of the abrasive gnoll language as the beasts communicated with one another across the forest. She realized that they must have been on a scouting or hunting mission when the jackal picked up her scent. Her troubles compounded again when she heard the sounds of fast-moving footsteps heading in the direction she was running.

She made a quick zigzag to the left and then the right, only to hear the same sounds on either side of her. She knew immediately that the four-legged demon-jackal had easily outdistanced her and gotten ahead so as to block her forward escape route. The slower nawgs broke off, one to the left and one to the right, preventing any escape in those directions. Her only option was to turn on her heel and go back the way she had come, but she realized after only a few steps that the wicked gnolls were approaching from that direction, covering that route as well. Surrounded, she knew she would be forced to fight, so she backed herself against one of the massive trees.

The first of the beasts stepped into the early evening light, cautiously snuffling at the air with its long black snout. She knew it immediately to be a nawg, and much bigger than she would have liked. The top of its head stood nearly five feet tall, and it resembled a hyena with a hint of boar mixed in. It had course, ruddy fur with black splotches along its back and rear haunches. Muscular and generally wedge-shaped, with massive shoulders and an arched back that tapered down to its well-muscled hind quarters, it had a black mane of bristling hair that circled around its neck and continued down its spine in a short crest that ended at the middle of its back.

The beast looked her way and seemed to laugh in an unnatural manner, brandishing its teeth and long tusks. Then its twin emerged from the opposite side of the scrub brush and scratched at the ground, waiting to see what would happen next.

Not long after, the demon-jackal came around

the backside of the tree, giving the nawgs a wide berth. The creature resembled a very large wild dog, except that it was a deep red color. It dropped its head and growled, bearing its teeth and sending a cold chill down Kestrel's spine. It watched her with malevolent eyes that gleamed with a terrifying, unquenchable hunger.

The gnolls were the last to arrive, walking upright on their hind legs, side by side, and carrying long barbed spears. Slightly taller than a human, they appear to be an evolutionary step—a missing link, as it were—between a hyena and a man. They had gray fur with reddish-gray manes and small, yellow-and-black spots covering most of their bodies. Both gnolls wore unkempt armor of leather and steel that covered their chests and upper, canine-like legs.

Kestrel had never seen gnolls and nawg associating together, but she knew in no uncertain terms that they were closely related. The fiercely independent demon-jackal was another story altogether, and why it had allied itself with the likes of those two was still a mystery. After witnessing the power that the Faerie Queen had just displayed, Kestrel had little doubt that it too was under her spell.

For a long moment Kestrel and her adversaries stared each other down, wondering who would blink first. Like their hunting companions, the gnolls were under the spell of the Faerie Queen and were trying to determine if this elf was an ally or a foe. The wild tribes of the Park despised the elves, and in the end their hatred won out: she was the enemy.

Kestrel knew that she wouldn't be able to deceive them. The powerful spell that controlled the beasts did not seem to be affecting her, and she knew that they understood this, as well. If it was magic that told them so or just a natural hatred for the goodly races, she would never know, but this wasn't the time to work that out.

Kestrel would have preferred to shoot them with her powerful bow, that being her usual weapon of choice, but her enemies were simply too close. She might get off one, maybe two shots, but the others would be on top of her before she could defend herself. Instead she drew her sword in one hand and held a long dagger in the other.

The finely polished elven blade of the sword shimmered with a thin hint of gold along its single edge. Technically the weapon would be considered a scimitar—a shamshir, to be exact. The sleek blade was long and relatively thin, slightly wider at its base and tapered at the tip. It extended in a shallow curve, similar to a samurai sword, with an unadorned sharkskin grip that ended in a long, swept-back, almost weightless pommel.

She allowed herself to slip into a state of mental awareness that would let her react on an instinctual level. The young elf scout hated to fight, but when it was necessary she was good…very good indeed.

Before she could make her first move, a scratching sound overhead caught her attention, and she dared look up for just an instant. What she saw was a welcome sight…but her attackers saw the squirrel, too. No longer hesitant, they came at her in a rush, with teeth and claws and long, barbed spears.

In an instant her sword was back in its sheath, and she squatted down, mentally sending strength into her legs. Just as she was about to jump, she hurled her dagger at the closest gnoll. It slammed into the beast's shin and tore into his unprotected leg, tripping him up and knocking him to the ground. As luck would have it, the second gnoll, only a step behind, couldn't stop and avoid its fallen companion. It collided with the prostrate brute, which sent it face-first into the ground, as well.

This bought the elf scout the few seconds she needed to escape. From a crouch, she leapt upward with all her might and threw herself nearly fifteen feet in the air with arms outstretched. She managed to grasp the cinch rigged around her squirrel, and the intelligent creature let her pull herself into the saddle as it turned and climbed higher into the tree. As they ascended, she watched while the nawgs and the demon-jackal clawed at the tree, snarling and growling with frustration after losing their prey.

-Chapter Six-

Poison Arrow

It had been nearly a week since the robbery at the museum when Commander Devin Crashblade found himself in the Park on the 13th level of the vast city of Cloudview. In the village of Tameral, a day's journey from the Park's entrance, he found a community of sylvan elves that considered themselves guardians of the Park. Their village was built high in the enormous treetops, but unlike their brethren in the Great Forest who built their vast empire within the canopy by manipulating the forest to their own design, the sylvan elves had chosen to let their living forest dictate how their community evolved.

Their homes and buildings were wrapped around the massive trees in a spiraling array of architectural beauty. Every structure was linked to another with a series of suspension bridges that spanned the gaps between each tree and the next. So perfectly balanced was the construction that, even though the community was quite large, it imparted minimal impact on the surrounding forest. Commander Crashblade admired the sheer beauty of the village and surrounding terrain, but the urgency of the situation had allowed him little time to dwell on it.

Crashblade was in the town's meeting hall surrounded by personal friends. Enob—the High Wizard of the Elf Nation of Greylok, located in the Great Forest outside Cloudview—stood to his left. He was accompanied by Fox Strongbow, the most recently appointed member of their King's elite guardians, known as Sentinels. To his right stood young Justin Kasey Hobskin and his talking wolf-dog partner, Murdox. The two of them were the detectives from Cloudview's Incantation Enforcement Agency who handled its Counter-Curse Division. All of them had worked together before on previous cases, except for one individual. The sixth person present was an elderly sylvan elf who was the spokesman for the local community.

Enob coughed into his fist to quiet down the room and give himself an opportunity to speak. "Thank you all for coming here on such short notice. I'm sorry to say that I'm once again the bearer of bad news." He paused for a moment to make sure he had everyone's attention. "I have recently discovered the truth behind the theft of the Sídhe relic and its relevance regarding a potentially dire situation. I'm afraid that the great multileveled city of Cloudview is in imminent peril, and we must make haste to rectify the situation."

The elderly spokesman for the village was the first to speak. "What might this have to do with us and, more specifically, with the Park?" He hesitated and then asked. "Does this have something to do with the power outage a few days ago?"

Enob looked at him for a moment and then replied, "I believe this has everything to do with the Park. I have learned that the Faerie Queen has taken possession of her people's most precious relic. She has obtained one of two staves crafted from the First Tree. Since I learned that the staff had been stolen, I've devoted my time to understanding its significance and discerning how to read the runes etched on its surface. Eventually I learned what should have been obvious to me from the beginning."

He paused for a moment to gather his thoughts and scan the circle of anxious faces before continuing. "I'll cut right to the point. The staff, in the hands of the Queen, is a device to re-grow the First Tree. It is essentially a seed, and I'm fairly certain that the power surge was the catalyst needed to initiate the Tree's regeneration."

"What does this mean?" asked the sylvan-elf spokesman.

Enob looked around the room, making certain he still had everyone's full attention. "This kind of event has never happened before. The power-draw required to black out all of Cloudview is unimaginable. The Faerie Queen somehow channeled the energy of the entire metropolis into the staff and thereby sparked life into the seed. I believe that the Tree will grow at an extremely accelerated rate, eventually using the energy of the city to break through the floor of the Park. Its roots will descend rapidly to the ground below

Cloudview, and it will then draw strength from the core of the world. I dare say that if this happens, we won't be able to stop it, and it will soon encompass and overwhelm the entire metropolis."

The room was silent for several moments as everyone considered Enob's words.

"What can we do to stop it?" asked the village elder.

Murdox harrumphed and replied, "Weed killer."

Crashblade suppressed a chuckle and thought about the history of the two detectives. Long ago Agent Murdox had himself been a wizard, but after a disastrous confrontation with an evil witchdoctor, he had been cursed to live the rest of his life as a wolf-dog. His partner at the time was Brent Hobskin, who was Kase's father. Brent had essentially sacrificed his very existence trying to protect Murdox from the curse. In the attempt, the full power of the hex had hit Kase's father pointblank, ripping his soul from him and changing him into a wolf.

Murdox and the agency had done what they could to bring Brent back to his former self, but nothing had worked. In the end the curse was simply too strong to counter, and Brent had been sent to live his remaining years in the Park as a wild animal. Kase then took up the mantle of his dad's position in the small but critically important Counter-Curse Division and became Murdox's new partner. Many had thought that Murdox's surly personality had developed as a result of the events that took place that day, but his friends knew better: he had always been that way.

The door to the meeting hall suddenly burst open, and a road-weary young elf stepped through. She was perhaps sixteen or seventeen—about the same age as Fox and slightly older than Kase. She was dirty and looked exhausted, but beautiful nonetheless, with her long silver hair pulled back and hanging straight between her shoulder blades. Kestrel realized immediately that this wasn't the usual local gathering of elf advisors, and as she joined the group inside, she quickly felt somewhat uncomfortable about her dramatic entrance. Fortunately, her supple, finely crafted elven armor didn't make a sound as it bent and crimped with every movement, but the effect wasn't nearly as imposing as she had hoped, either.

As she entered, her expression was stern, and the emerald-green eyes that glistened in the candlelight revealed both her intelligence and the clear fact that she meant business. The community spokesman seemed slightly embarrassed about the intrusion, but his agitation quickly vanished when he saw the serious expression on her face.

"I would like to introduce Kestrel Greenleaf," he told the others. "She's one of our finest scouts and has been on an extended expedition well beyond our borders. From the look on her face, I'm betting she has some important news for all of us."

"I apologize for the interruption, but I've just returned from the edge of Myrr Wood and have witnessed a very disturbing sight."

Twenty minutes later she had relayed every detail of her encounter at the border of the Sídhe kingdom, including the strange power surge and the flash of green light. She described her encounter with the griffon, the army of fiends that ringed the forest boundary, and finally her near miss with the gnolls and their hunting companions. She had everyone's undivided attention throughout, and when she was finished, she was satisfied that they had absorbed every word.

Enob nodded in recognition. "As I feared, what I suspected might happen has come to pass."

They all looked at the wizard, hoping that he had some kind of solution to this mess. Justin Kasey Hobskin was the first to speak.

"Is there something we can do to stop it?" asked Kase, wondering where this new adventure would lead.

By a twist of fate, Kase and his father, a former New York City police detective, had originally traveled to Cloudview down a spiral staircase that they'd discovered descending from inside a magical chest. After arriving, they had tried to return to their own world but had found no means to do so. Finally Kase's father had obtained a job at the Incantation Enforcement Agency, and he and Murdox had founded the Counter Curse division and worked together until the fateful day when they'd encountered the witchdoctor, and the younger Hobskin had then taken on his father's role.

Although Kase was very young for an agent, and Murdox had been hexed, the new partnership actually worked out very well. In a world full of magic and a wide array of diverse creatures with their own agendas, no one paid much attention to a human boy and a dog, which made Kase and Murdox seem less threatening to both bureaucrats and perpetrators of crime. They performed their jobs admirably and were allowed to keep their division open. Their little office had actually saved the Agency a fortune in insurance claims while helping to solve numerous magical crimes, so no one wanted it shut down, regardless of who ran it.

Enob regarded the boy with respect, for Kase and his partner had within the last couple of years saved the life of the old wizard's monarch and helped foil an evil dragon's attempt to take over the world. "Yes. I believe there is something we can each do." Enob then looked to the local spokesman and the young scout. "Are you aware of the poison oaks?"

Both nodded in recognition.

"Yes," said the elf scout. "There is a small grove of the vile trees a few days journey from here."

"But it lies within a terrible bog from which few have ever returned," added the spokesman.

Murdox grumbled under his breath. "Did we expect anything less? Why couldn't it be...oh, I don't know...maybe on a beautiful tropical beach somewhere instead?"

Kase gave the wolf-dog a stern look and smiled weakly to the others. "Sorry about that. That's just his way of saying 'Sure, we're eager to provide any help you might need.'"

Murdox growled at the boy but said nothing more.

Enob smiled ever so slightly. "That is good news, for I know of another similar growth of trees, but it is many weeks' travel from here...and I fear that would be too late." The wizard looked around the group again and went on. "These trees are poisonous. I would suspect that their growth in that region is the cause of the bog's existence. Regardless, we need a branch from one of them, from which I can fabricate a poisoned arrow. If we can then transport the arrow to the Faerie kingdom before the Tree's roots reach the ground below Cloudview, I think it can destroy the Tree."

"Then it's decided," said the elf scout. "I can be ready in a couple of hours."

Enob looked at the circles under her eyes and the filth that covered her light armor. "I appreciate your enthusiasm, but we still have a few things to do first. It's probably been days since you've had a decent night's sleep, and I dare say that you're in need of a bath."

The wizard looked around the room again and focused his gaze on the elderly spokesman. "We will need to depart by morning. With you're approval, may we take our leave?"

The spokesman nodded without hesitation and left the room for just a moment to relay a message to one of the runners waiting outside the door. "I have just called for maps of the area and for provisions, armor, and of course transportation to take your company to the grove of poison oaks. You must take Kestrel with you. She's our finest scout and knows the lands better

Sidhe

than anyone." He looked over at the young ranger. "Go with the runner," he told her, "and once you have put the preparations in motion, get yourself cleaned up, and get some sleep. Tomorrow will be here soon enough.

The elf scout nodded and left the hall.

The spokesman looked at the young Sentinel and Enob for a moment and paused. "This mission is of the utmost importance to the entire city. I had understood that there were two Sentinels at Greylok. Why is the other not with you?"

For a long moment neither Fox nor Enob spoke. Finally a look of resignation came over Enob's face. "You speak of Eldin, but I'm afraid he is no longer able to carry the role of Sentinel. Not long ago while flying over the Swamp of Doom and Despair both Eldin and Fox were dragged from the sky by an evil black dragon. In a desperate battle between the dragon and the two Sentinels, Fox was knocked unconscious, and Eldin was brought near to death. The ancient dragon was also mortally wounded in the battle and, through primordial magic, its dark soul drifted out from its corporeal form and possessed the dying body of Eldin. The beast, inhabiting the form of Eldin, attempted to locate a powerful artifact so that it might gain great power."

The wizard gestured to the small group. "Assisted by agents Kase and Murdox, and myself, Fox thwarted his attempt and freed Eldin from the dragon's grasp. The ordeal left the senior Sentinel scarred—not in any physical way, but mentally. He hasn't been able to function sufficiently ever since. He fears that the evil that was inside him might resurface, and he can no longer serve in his previous role."

The spokesman gazed at Fox Strongbow for a moment. He knew of him well enough. He'd never before met the young elf, whose reputation had already preceded him at the highest levels. The spokesman looked him over, noting for the first time that he was about the same age as Kestrel. He was young indeed for an elf—sixteen, maybe seventeen years old—not even a drop in the bucket for their long-lived race.

Outwardly he looked like most elves: medium height, long black hair tied neatly behind his head, pointed ears, and a deceptively small frame. There was, however, something distinctly different about him, and

Sidhe

the spokesman pondered it for a second. Outwardly he was in perfect physical condition, but that wasn't what attracted the spokesman's attention. Rather it was the way he carried himself. He seemed casual and calm, but hidden below was the intensity of a tiger about to leap on its prey. In addition, his clear, gray eyes portrayed something rare: an intelligence and inner strength that the spokesman had seen in only two others. One had been Eldin and the other, Kestrel.

"I've heard rumors about Eldin's encounter for some time, but I had never been privy to the truth. Now, unfortunately, I know the real story," said the elderly elf. He looked back at Fox and went on. "I met your teacher many years ago, shortly after you began training with him. It was then believed that you were the first and only elf in ages to be born with the rare gift, the special abilities that permitted you to become a Sentinel, but in truth you were not. One other had been born a few months before you. She was here in this village, and Eldin gained knowledge of her existence. He came to us one day and visited with the girl. Her parents had been killed less than a year before, when a marauding band of orcs invaded our community."

He gazed around the room before continuing.

"Rather than send her away with Eldin, we elders adopted her as our own. I realized that here in the Park we did not have the means to train a Sentinel, but we did have other ways to develop the enormous power of her gift. Most important, after her personal struggle with the deaths of her parents, we didn't have the heart to send her off with complete strangers. How could we in good conscience abandon her to a lifetime of servitude to a king she hadn't even known existed?"

He waited a moment for the others to consider his words before he continued.

"We decided to take on the responsibility ourselves, and the best of our rangers and trackers trained her from an early age in the use of weapons and in forestry. Our finest scholars and wizards guided her in the development of her mind and helped her learn to use her gift to its full potential. Today she is a formidable weapons master, and I dare say she can shoot a bow better than anyone I have ever seen. As a ranger she has no equal."

Fox shook his head in total surprise. After Eldin's falling, he had been truly concerned that he would find no equal partner and could only seek out an apprentice to train...if an appropriate one could ever be found. To learn that someone else had been born with the gift and had already mastered the use of it to any great degree was a small miracle in itself. The fact that this someone was a girl his own age was also remarkable.

"This is fantastic! I'm truly glad to hear this news. I was concerned that, aside from Eldin, I might be the only elf in the world with these abilities."

The spokesman was pleased that Fox did not allow his own ego to get in the way of what could be a very valuable relationship. He also felt relief and satisfaction regarding his decisions about Kestrel's training and her well-being.

The door to the meeting room then opened, and two young runners entered, bringing with them a large platter of food and a few neatly rolled maps. They set out everything on a banquet table in front of the group. Murdox didn't hesitate to attack the food, completely ignoring the rest of the party. Kase quickly grabbed him by the collar and dragged him away from the table.

"Hey! Save some for the rest of us!"

Murdox smiled in the way that only a dog can and, in the process, dropped a half-eaten turkey leg to the floor.

"Fine," he agreed. "I'll listen in on the conversation."

Kase had hardly turned around before the wolf-dog was back at the table, stuffing his face. The young agent was about to pull him away again when Enob pushed aside the platter to make room on the table for the maps.

They all gleaned what they could from the drawings and together chose what appeared to be the best route to the bog.

"We will provide you with three owls for transport to the edge of the bog," said the elf spokesman as he wondered privately about the wolf-dog, who had blueberry pie all over his muzzle. "There they will wait in safety for your return. The creatures are very intelligent, and once the poison arrow is fabricated, they will be a great asset for traveling quickly and silently to the Sídhe kingdom. If you are to succeed in this mission, you will have to employ all your skills to slip undiscovered through the dark forest surrounding the faerie kingdom. With news that an army is guarding the forest, I fear the job will be all the more difficult."

Kase looked at the map and then over to the spokesman. "Why can't the birds fly over the bog?"

The elf spokesman looked at the boy quizzically, as though the answer should have been obvious. Then Murdox, gulping a mouthful of pie, spoke up before he could reply.

"Think back to when we were in the Swamp of Doom and Despair. It's a lot like that. The area is just a vast wasteland of evil fiends. Dragons and other vile winged creatures hunt the land continuously for food. The owls rely on the cover of trees, rolling hills, or mountains for stealth, and the bog is barren, but for a few scrub trees and a scattering of low-lying boulders. With no cover, they would be easy prey for the larger and more dangerous beasts that inhabit the area."

One Wizard Place

Commander Crashblade nodded. "The owls are key players in this campaign. There'd be too much risk of losing one of them and further endangering yourselves in the process."

The spokesman once again took the floor. "The area where you will leave the birds is a large, rocky outcropping in the foothills of a mountain that is seemingly uncontaminated by the poison of the bog. It juts out into the wasteland considerably but still allows the birds a measure of protection. In addition it gives you a head start to the poison oaks, which are only a day's march from there. Including your trek through the bog, you should reach the Sídhe kingdom within a week or so." He looked over to Enob for confirmation, and the wizard spoke.

"It should take me just a few hours to construct the arrow from a tree branch…so I agree with your conclusion." The wizard looked over the small company and continued, "I will only accompany you through the bog and make our return to the owls. From what I have learned about the growth of the Tree, my services will be of much more use in the city at that point. I'll use my magic to hinder the development of the roots and buy as much time as I can for you to complete the mission."

Commander Crashblade nodded his head in agreement. "My services will also be of greater use in the city. Inevitably there will be panic in the streets, and it will take every available member of the Agency to keep it under control."

The spokesman looked them over with a measure of respect, sizing up each one of them. "Then it is settled. Kestrel, Fox, Kase, and Murdox will be our heroes for this undertaking. The birds can easily accommodate two riders: Kestrel and Kase will travel in tandem, while Murdox will ride behind Fox on a second owl. Enob will be carried alone on the third owl and will return here after fashioning the arrow, and our champions will continue their journey to the Sídhe."

-Chapter Seven-
Yellow Eyes

The following morning came far too quickly. The sun still hadn't broken the horizon when the five companions found themselves standing in front of a large roost where the birds were housed. Commander Crashblade had left the evening before, returning to the urban levels of Cloudview to help keep the peace, and the sylvan elf community's spokesman was probably still sleeping comfortably in his bed. All the preparations for the journey had been made the night before, and everything they needed was already waiting for them.

Murdox sniffed at the air and scrunched up his nose. "Big birds mean big... poo...."

Kase gave the wolf-dog a stern look and kneed him lightly in the ribs.

Kestrel smiled and then walked to the large,

wooden door and pushed it open. "I doubt the owls are asleep. They probably heard us coming from a mile away."

The door creaked opened, and six large eyes glowed faintly in the early morning light. Kestrel lit a torch that hung on one of the walls, illuminating the room so that they all could see inside it. The glowing orbs blinked in unison, and the little company realized that they too were being watched.

The first owl rotated its head around to get a better look at the companions. It was a huge creature with a large, rounded head and beautiful feathers the color of snow. Its white chest was spotted with dark gray patches that extended around its back and onto its tail feathers. The creature let out a soft whistle, turning its head away from the group after deciding they weren't a threat.

The second owl was slightly larger than the first, with long ear tufts that extended upward from its head. It was a deep brown with mottled gray and white streaks that set off a nearly pure white throat. The feathers on its head came to a point, separating two semi-circular black rings that surrounded its intelligent eyes.

The third creature, at the back of the owlery, was by far the largest of the three. It was densely plumaged with a large, heart-shaped facial disk and bright yellow eyes. The upper half of the bird was a dusky gray above a dark belly that was spotted with fine white dots. It made a deep *whoo!* as the companions approached, but otherwise it paid them little attention.

The birds watched as the little group made their way to the back of the room. Kestrel nudged Fox and pointed to a bolted door just beyond the last owl. "If you'll get out the riding gear," she prompted, "I'll lead the birds to the launching area."

Fox nodded without comment and unbolted the door to the storage room.

The elf scout first took hold of the snowy owl's tether and led the bird out of the building. She returned a minute later to direct the two remaining birds from their roost and lead them to the middle of a large, hay-covered deck that extended outward from the tree. Fox

Sidhe

and Enob followed after her, carrying two huge saddles. Kase came right behind them with an armful of leather harnesses and flight clothing.

They each piled their gear next to an owl and began to saddle the birds. Having flown on a falcon for many years, Fox had no trouble helping Kestrel and Enob prepare the creatures for flight. It took a little work, but in less than an hour the job was complete. They gave the saddles a final check and secured their heavily laden flight packs for the trip.

"Fox, you and Murdox should take the horned owl," Kestrel suggested. "I'll carry Kase with me on the great gray, and Enob should take the snowy owl."

Fox nodded his approval and gently approached the head of his owl so the creature could give him a thorough once-over. "If it's okay, the wolf-dog and I will be riding with you on this little adventure."

The bird sniffed at his hand and allowed the young man to touch him on the beak, creating an instant bond between the two. Like Kestrel, Fox had a way with the creatures of the world and seemingly could communicate with them on a subconscious level.

Murdox, however, wasn't so lucky, and the bird sniffed at him with a distasteful look in its eyes.

Murdox stuck his nose in the air and looked away. "*Humph!* I don't want to do this any more than you do. From the sound of it, though, I don't think either one of us has any choice in the matter, so you're just going to have to deal with it."

The bird looked to Kestrel and Fox, but both of them just shrugged in response. Finally the owl conceded the point and nudged Murdox in the side in an almost polite gesture. The wolf-dog grunted in response, apparently not very happy that he would have to go after all.

Yellow streaks of light slipped through the dense canopy of the forest as the three birds lined up for takeoff. Kestrel, with Kase seated behind her, was first off the deck, followed by Enob and finally Fox and Murdox, taking up the rear. Their owls silently leapt into the air, gliding on the morning currents and into the dim light of the forest.

By early afternoon the party was making good time and took a short break to rest the birds and grab a quick bite to eat. Kestrel removed the map from her flight pack and determined where they were.

"We're doing well for time. If we push the birds, I think we can make the edge of the bog by early evening. We'll rest and get a fresh start across in the morning. There isn't a really good map of the area, but over the years I've tried to piece together what I could. The place is treacherous and, for the most part, a wasteland saturated with fetid marshes and stagnant, algae-covered pools."

"Sounds like a nice place to spend a few days," Murdox commented with a snarl.

Kase gave the wolf-dog a dirty sidelong glance. "How are we going to get across when we're so exposed to predators?"

Kestrel smiled ever so slightly. "It's not going to be easy, but I managed to procure some concealment cloaks." The elf girl glanced over at Fox. "They're hardly as good as his, but they should keep us relatively concealed from aerial predators. We'll stay low and try our best to use what little vegetation we can find to keep hidden."

She studied the map for a moment more. "If I estimate the distance correctly, and we keep a decent pace, we should reach the dead forest by early evening. There we'll set watch and rest until morning."

"Sounds like a walk in the Park...no pun intended," chimed in Murdox.

Kase snickered a little too late and with a sarcastic emphasis. "I get it: "Park"—we're actually in the Park."

He got a queer look from the group, but they all got a good laugh out of it.

Shortly thereafter they were back on wing, flying between the trunks of the forest as much as possible until it became too dense to weave between the trees. They had a few hours left and resolved to skim over the treetops, keeping as low as possible in the hope of avoiding unwanted attention from above.

By the time the sun started to swing down toward the horizon, they were approaching a range of dark, rugged mountains that they had been watching ever since they'd left the protection of the forest. Kase looked up at the tall peaks and crags overhead. They reminded him of a European film set. Though he had never been to the mountains in Transylvania, he had seen them on late night horror movies that he and his father watched before they had landed in this strange stairway world.

Kestrel slowed her bird and circled back, signaling for the others to follow. They landed in a small field just within the foothills of the mountain range.

The elf girl guided her bird close enough to the others that they all might hear. She glanced over at Fox and Enob and grimaced. "I don't much like the look of these mountains, but from all the maps it seems we're on the right course. I spotted a small ravine that seemed to cut between the crags, but I didn't get a good feeling about it."

Enob looked up at the tall, black mountains in front of them and shook his head. "I feel that we shouldn't fly over the top, since it will expose us to the predators that live up there. I don't doubt that a few dragons make a home of this vile place, just waiting for a tasty morsel to fly right onto their doorsteps."

Fox looked toward the dark ravine and winced. "I'm sure you're right about that, but I have a feeling that canyon isn't much safer. This is a lose-lose situation, if I ever saw one."

There was little choice. Flying over the canyon undoubtedly posed the greatest danger, but flying through it would probably be no picnic either.

The elf girl looked over the little group. "I have no idea what's in there. We'll just have to keep up our guard and hope for the best."

Anticipating some kind of snide remark from Murdox, Kase waggled his finger at the wolf-dog and stared him down.

"What…?" said Murdox with a pained look on his doggy face.

Kestrel launched her owl first, followed by Enob's and Fox's birds. They climbed about a hundred feet in the air and headed straight into the canyon. Even at that height, the canyon walls loomed far overhead, with only a thin strip of blue sky marking the upper edge. Gliding silently on the gentle currents of wind, they pushed onward, hoping to avoid obstacles.

Hardly discernable to any but the most sensitive of ears, a sound awoke the creature. Two red eyes opened, quickly adjusting to the darkness of the cave. It listened intently to the sounds that floated on the gentle currents of air that drifted through the cavern. It sensed a vibration, an almost indiscernible change in pressure that made its bat-like ears hum. Releasing its claws from the ceiling, the beast dropped to the cavern floor.

The monster was a demonic abomination. Outwardly it appeared to be a fusion of a bat and a man. It stood upright on two spindly legs, with claws for feet. Coarse black hair covered its body, and small, leathern wings extended from beneath its long arms.

Vampire-like, it fed on the blood of warm-blooded creatures. Only at night was it at its full strength, and only in the darkness could it see. Early evening was approaching, and it was almost time to feed. Unlike with true vampires, the sun would not destroy this close cousin, but it preferred not to roam far from the safety of its cavern during the daylight hours.

Not yet proven amongst its kind, this one had been assigned as a scout. Every evening its mission was to find food for its brethren, who dwelled deeper in the vast cavern. Every day it hoped that a meal was about to fly by.

Over centuries of evolution, these creatures had lost the ability to fly. Their meager wings allowed them only to glide short distances, relying primarily on enormous bats that they used for aerial transport.

The fiend made its way to where the bats roosted, finding one just beginning to stir from the scent of its approaching master. The bat released its claws from the ceiling, spreading wide its leathery wings and gliding out into the cavern. The vampire made a clucking sound with its tongue, signaling for creature to return.

Hardly slowing, the bat raced low over the cavern floor, stopping only moments before reaching its master. The vampire grabbed hold of a leather reign and slung itself into the saddle. Immediately the bat took to wing and accelerated away from the ground. It weaved and turned between the stalactites, quickly gaining speed before exiting the cavern.

There was still a least an hour of daylight left, but the sun had already dipped below the rim of the canyon, casting the ravine into shadows. Almost instantly the vampire sensed the proximity of the prey ahead of it. Using its keen senses, it was able to determine their location, and it took up pursuit. Without its brethren it dared not get close enough to put them on guard. Its job was simply to follow and determine if they would be suitable for the needs of its clan.

The hair on the back of Fox's neck stood on end. He sensed that danger was near and readied his bow. The young Sentinel steered his owl as close as he could to Kestrel's bird. "Something's tailing us," he called.

Kestrel nodded and patted the quiver of arrows at her side. She slowed her bird and came up beside Enob. "Be ready—we're being followed."

Enob looked all around him, but couldn't see any pursuit.

Kestrel smiled. "Trust us."

The vampire spotted its prey far below. The sound of the three beating hearts of the birds sent it into a raging blood lust. Its charge was to scout out potential food sources, but with the sound of all that pumping blood, any sensible thoughts fled from its mind. It knew that the birds carried riders, but this meant little to it. It pressed its steed forward, urging the bat to dive at the birds. The bat, however, had some sense left and resisted its master's command. The vampire would have none of it and pressed harder until, reluctantly, the bat gave in to its will and dove downward.

The bat was on a collision course, headed right for the little group. They all saw it coming, but it was still far enough above them to allow them to react. In unison the three birds peeled away. Fox went to the right, Kestrel dove to the left, and Enob fell behind. Fox and Kestrel then steadied their bows, aiming for a clear shot.

Kestrel fired first, hitting the bat squarely in the chest and causing the creature to veer sideways. This opened up a shot for Fox, and he released his arrow. It made contact with the bat, tearing a hole through the thin membrane of one of its wings.

Furious that its dinner would be no simple matter to claim, the vampire released the bat from the dive. This allowed the creature to turn away from the next volley of arrows and narrowly miss a shot aimed at its head. The violent maneuver took it dangerously close to the canyon walls and, as a result, it managed to slip below the flight path of the owls.

Still overcome with bloodlust, the vampire pulled on the reins of its bat, forcing the creature to climb. It hoped to attack from below and avoid the deadly arrows of the two archers.

Fox and Kestrel yanked their birds sideways and fired off another volley of arrows at the bat. The creature narrowly avoided the missiles and continued to climb uncomfortably fast, right towards them.

A glowing ball of flame formed in Enob's hand, and with a sly smile he casually tossed it downward next to his bird. The fireball fell harmlessly for a few seconds, seemingly of little danger to the approaching creature. Enob gave a quick wink to Kestrel and snapped his fingers. At that moment the fireball stopped instantly in mid air and hovered in place. Enob waved his hand to the side, and it accelerated like a guided missile directly toward the bat and its demonic rider.

Neither the vampire nor the bat had any time to react. The fireball slammed into them, instantly engulfing them in flame. The vampire lost control of the bat, and the whole smoking conflagration fell toward the ground. Enob snapped his fingers once more, and the flames instantly dispersed, re-forming as the ball of fire a few feet away from the falling creature.

To the vampire's credit, it was able to bring the bat back under control and make a hard landing on the floor of the canyon. Still smoking from their encounter with the fireball, both creatures were amazed that they were somehow still alive. Most of the hair on both the vampire and its bat had been singed and was still smoldering, but they would live to fight another day. For a brief second the vampire looked up toward the sky and considered regaining the chase. It found only a small glowing ball of flame, hovering just a few feet overhead, and decided that maybe it wasn't worth a try, after all. It would let this meal get away.

By twilight the small party spotted the desolate bog ahead of them, and each rider instinctively cringed at the sight. Even the beauty of the setting sun, as it disappeared below the horizon in a wave of orange light, couldn't mask the treacherous land that lay before them.

-Chapter Eight-

The Bog

The little party had spent a fretful night camped on a long rock pinnacle that jutted out from the mountain's foothills. As planned, their owls were gone, dismissed before their presence would attract any predators. In the morning they congregated at the edge of the neck of land, viewing the vast wasteland of bog ahead of them. The sky was dark, thick with storm clouds. The sun must have been shining far overhead, but the only light that could penetrate the clouds was gray, and the day was gloomy and cold.

Directly in front of them was the edge of a small black pool of stagnant water, but this was not the only such pool they saw. There were thousands of them, one every few yards, for as far as the eye could see. At this moment the bog was quiet, but they could feel anger in the air, as if at any moment it could come alive and strike them down.

A narrow, muddy path stretched out ahead of them. It weaved and wound through the pools in a maze-like fashion, disappearing far off in the distance.

Kase took a good look around before commenting.

"Dreary morning, I would say."

Murdox walked to the edge of the rocky base and put a paw down onto the muddy path. A drop of brown rain fell from the sky and landed on his head.

"You don't say," he countered.

The company broke camp and gathered together their packs.

Kestrel tried to smile, but couldn't.

"I suppose we had better get this over with."

A collective groan issued from the company, but everyone complied.

They lined up on the edge of the rock. Kestrel was the first, followed by Enob, Kase, Murdox, and Fox taking up the rear. One by one they stepped into the mud.

For hours they followed the meandering path as it weaved between the stagnant pools, with little to show for it. Ahead of them the horizon hardly changed; all they could see was more mud.

For what seemed like the hundredth time Kestrel stepped down, and her leg went knee deep into the mud. With a sucking sound, she pulled it out and moaned. "Will this vile place never end?" She led them around the muddy pit and reluctantly continued in the direction the path seemed to be leading.

A splash in a pool behind them caught them off guard. In anticipation of a fight, Fox and Kestrel reached for their swords, but a slight ripple in the pool was all that remained. To this point, nothing had bothered them. The only life they had seen was the occasional mud-encrusted rat darting across the path. A few times, far off in the distance, they'd heard a howl or a wail that alluded to greater danger lurking about, but as of yet all had remained quiescent for them. A couple of strained minutes passed, but nothing further happened.

Kestrel pushed forward, and all was well for the

next few hours. By midafternoon they were wet and weary from struggling through the thick mud. They wanted to rest, but without shelter they feared to stop for more than a few minutes.

Another splash stopped them in their tracks, followed by another and another. At first they saw only a vague outline of what was below the water. Then suddenly it leapt from the pool, flying over the path and disappearing into the blackness of another pool.

Its long, serpentine body bounded from one pool to the next. It was huge and not particularly friendly looking. The creature was primarily black, with an opaque green crest that ran along its spine and a set of fins near its head. Its was so long that as it jumped from one pool to the next, the end of its body remained in one and sometimes two pools at once, trailing behind in an oscillating wave. Its final jump took it over the heads of the companions as it dove into the pool closest to them. Hunger smoldered in its glowing orange eyes as it smiled at the group with a mouthful of needle-like teeth.

In the blink of an eye, both Fox and Kestrel had

their weapons in hand, as the creature weaved back and forth in front of them. Before it could attack, however, a small bird flew in front of the beast, leaving in its wake a cloud of black powder that drifted right into the serpents face. The bog beast inhaled the dust and shook its head as it began sneezing uncontrollably.

In the confusion the bird circled around Murdox's head, whispering into the wolf-dog's ear. "Within the boundary of the poison oaks, look for a large tree in the shape of a Y. In the roots is a small cave. Get there before the sun sets, and you should be safe. Stay to the trail and you'll find it."

A moment later the voice was gone, leaving Murdox with a ringing in his ear. *I really have to stay away from all that rich food,* he chided himself.

The beast soon lost interest in the small band of heroes and dove back into the inky, black pool, completely disappearing from sight. Murdox contemplated the message and relayed the information to his friends. Under the circumstances no one objected, and they took off at a run.

Dusk came, and the shadows were at their

longest. The small band of travelers had nearly reached the boarder of the poison oaks when, far too close, came the sound of the night creatures. If the bog wasn't at all pleasant during the day, it was at least relatively free from wandering predators. The night was an altogether different story. Evil roamed the bog after sunset, and the table was set for an evening meal.

The sky darkened, and the shadows started to ripple and roil. The foulest of beasts woke from their daytime slumber and crawled from the stench of their dens. With popping and squishing sounds, desiccated hands reached out of the mud and groped for the companions' legs. One hand grabbed the wolf-dog, and he howled in furry, kicking at the appendage until it released its grip.

All around them the muddy ground swelled and popped. Grotesque humanoid creatures pulled themselves free of the restricting mud and crawled onto the path. They resembled corpses with wild, hungry eyes and with leathery skin drawn tight across partially visible bones. The party took off in a run, easily outdistancing the slowly rambling creatures.

Sidhe

Not fifty steps later, a deathly cry rang across the bog, stopping the group in their tracks. In the dim light they spotted wild packs of catlike creatures racing toward the ghoulish figures. There were too many to count, and moving at an alarmingly fast pace. In a wave of destruction, the group swelled over the ghouls, bringing them to the ground. The wild pack of felines dragged the ghouls down the path, swarming over the hapless creatures and tearing into them.

Hardly audibly, Murdox whimpered, and a hundred malevolent red eyes looked away from their meals and spotted the companions standing there. Almost all claws and teeth, the small, catlike creatures had shabby brown fur and bristling manes of short quills. Individually they might pose little threat, but an organized horde of this size would tear through the small party as easily as they annihilated the ghouls.

Not waiting around to see what would happen next, the companions sprinted away down the path. As one, the horde sized up these new, interesting creatures and decided that if they could move, they were probably fit to eat. One by one they began to yowl until the sound became almost deafening. The message was loud and clear to the little party: *Run faster!*

The horde had almost caught up with them when they reached the edge of the poison oaks. A skeletal forest of deadly giant trees stretched out before them, but with a pack of carnivorous cats hot on their trail, they had little time to take in the sights. Murdox spotted the Y-shaped tree first and raced to it. Blindly he dove between the roots and was pleased to find that the small cave there didn't have any occupants.

He tumbled into the void and rolled as far away from the entrance as he could. Kase, Enob, Kestrel, and Fox followed directly behind him. Instantly, Fox and Kestrel had their weapons in hand, taking a stance at the opening to the cave. In silence they waited and watched the black void, shifting their vision to the infrared spectrum. They expected to see hundreds of warm bodies just outside their hollow, but to their surprise they could see only the cooling outlines of the skeletal forest surrounding them. With great stealth Fox and Kestrel climbed out of the cave, ready for anything, but again they were surprised to find only silence.

Perched deep in the shadows of a low-lying branch not far away, a small, black raven watched it all. The bird kept its keen eyes on the scene, as the final rays of sunlight slipped below the horizon, casting the bog in complete darkness.

For more than an hour the companions huddled in the darkness of the cave. Nothing disturbed them there, but out of fear they kept silent and dared not light a fire.

Murdox's stomach was the first to give in, and the wolf-dog nudged Kase with his cold nose.

"Look, I don't think those confused house cats followed us into the forest. I'm thinking it's okay to have a little light and maybe a nice bit of dinner," said Murdox in a whisper.

Kase shook his head in frustration and touched Kestrel on the shoulder. "What do you think? Is it alright to eat and maybe get some rest?"

Kestrel shrugged and peered into the darkness. "I don't see anything at the moment. My night vision would pick up the heat signature of anything warm out there, especially living creatures. All I can see is the dim glow of everything cooling down from the warmth of the day." She turned to Fox. "How about you?"

The young Sentinel shook his head. "Nope, I can't make out anything either, but I do have an eerie, almost foreboding feeling about this place."

Enob looked to the mouth of the cave. "I'm pretty sure we all share the same feelings, but we do need to keep up our strength—we have a long way to go."

"No problem," said Kase as he pulled open the flap of his backpack. "I think I've got something in here that should help."

A few moments later he illuminated the cavern with a lantern that looked far too big to have fit into his bag. Kestrel was confounded, but no one else seemed to notice that anything was out of the ordinary. Just as she was about to say something, the young agent produced an enormous steak and bowl of water for Murdox, a large wrapped plate of fruit and cheese, a huge loaf of bread, a jug full of ice tea, and four mugs for the group.

The boy smiled at Kestrel, noticing the look on her face. "I'd like to explain how it works, but trying to understand or explain quantum-dimensional spaces always gives me a headache."

Kestrel just shrugged in agreement; after all she was living in the Park, which was nothing more than an immense quantum-dimensional space. How else could you fit an entire continent into a space the size of even a large city?

Quietly they dug into the food, eating their fill until no one could complain of being hungry...not even Murdox. The cave they were in wasn't big by any standards. It appeared to have been a cavity created by the tree's roots as they dug deep into the soft ground in search of water. Like the rest of the trees in the dead forest, this one was nothing more than a hollow shell, produced as years of decay took its toll on the once-proud oaks.

Kase looked over to Kestrel. "What has happened to this land and poisoned these trees?"

Kestrel shook her head. "Honestly, I'm not sure."

Enob scratched at the floor with a long stick, scrawling little lines in the dirt. "I've been thinking about why the cat creatures didn't follow us into the forest, and I think it must tie into the legend of the poisoned oaks. As the legend goes, dryads used to protect these forests. You see dryads are wild creatures of the earth that live deep in the woodlands, guarding the trees from those who would fell them and steal the wood. Their bodies and skin are almost wood-like, and their hair is made of leaves, like the canopy of the trees they protect. Very rarely, a dryad looses interest in her trees, and vanity overcomes her. She desires to become mortal and walk the earth as a woman of flesh and blood."

He hesitated for a moment, gathering his thoughts, and then went on. "That in itself is probably not the rarest of things, but in the case of this poisoned grove, and only one other I am aware of, something else has happened. You see, these creatures are solitary in nature, each usually guarding no more than a hundred trees within their territory. Rarely do they stray from their beloved charges and congregate among their own kind as a group. That's what makes this event so strange. One of these creatures must have turned from her given life and somehow convinced others of her kind to join in her way of thinking. They allowed their trees to be cut down and taken away so that they in turn could buy themselves mortality."

Kase looked confused. "How can you buy mortality?"

Enob stirred the dirt some more with his feet. "Dryads are nothing more than elves that long, long ago gave up their original physical forms to become closer to the trees. Over time they became one with the earth and protectors of the land. However, a powerful wizard does have the ability to change a dryad back into an elf. It's very dark magic, and only a handful of black-hearted wizards could possibly accomplish such a task. The magic alone kills the land, extracting the nutrients from the ground to accomplish the transformation. A wizard that would do such a thing would demand an astronomical fee."

He looked around at the faces of his companions and saw that they were all listening with rapt attention. "Thus the evil circle begins. The dryads allow their forest to be stripped in exchange for money to pay the wizard, and that begins the travesty. More than just money is required for the transformation to take place. For the magic to work, they must entomb one of their own kind in the largest and proudest tree within their protection. They use her magic to pull the life force from the ground, slowly killing all that surrounds the tree. The turned dryads use this energy to fuel their life force, keeping themselves young and beautiful. Their deed poisons the tree, and the poison leaches out across the surrounding land."

He shook his head and continued. "This is where the lore ends, and I have to speculate what happens next. Once the land is stripped of its life force, the magic falls away. The toll of mortality must be paid, and the dryads begin to age and eventually die. Their dark souls cannot pass from this world, and I believe the earth binds them to what they have destroyed."

Kestrel looked out into the darkness beyond the opening to their cave. The moon was only a sliver in the sky, and the surrounding wood was black. "I can sense the hatred and doom that surrounds this place. I feel that what you say is the truth."

Fox picked up the lantern and moved closer to the entrance of the small cave, letting the light shine into the darkness. For the rest of his days, he would never forget what he saw that night. Enob was right. The spirits of the dryads wandered between the trees. Their spectral remains were stuck between the land of the living and the world of shadows. Their deeds in life prevented them passage to the Land of the Dead, and their souls were trapped in this decayed forest.

The elves believe that if the soul of the deceased is not pure, then it returns to the land of the living in the guise of a ghost. As long as the soul is not freed from negative emotions such as greed, vanity, or anger, the ghost will remain.

The black souls of the dryads had no right to pass into a peaceful afterlife. Their punishment was condemnation to the woods that they had desecrated, and they haunted the place with a madness all their own.

On seeing them Fox felt their hatred, fear, and hunger, as all their accumulated emotions poured into his soul. They stared at the young Sentinel from empty eye sockets and drifted toward him like creatures in a nightmare. Fox slipped back into the cave as white as a sheet, shivering with fear.

"*Yyesss*...I believe you're right."

Outside the cave they heard the moans and wailing of the dryad ghosts, hungry for a taste of the living.

"Why haven't they come after us?" asked Kase as he pushed himself as far back into the cave as he could.

Enob listened to the cries. "I believe they're stopped by the trees. They've been bound to this place because of what they did to the land. Long before vanity overcame them, they loved and nurtured these trees. Now in death they are ashamed of what they did in life and are filled with too much humiliation to approach what they've killed. I think we should be safe while we're in here."

Up in the branches of the dead tree, the raven ruffled its feathers and placed its head under a wing.

Chapter Nine

Wailing Spirits

Morning came after a restless night in the cave. Each member of the party had taken a watch, but few had gotten any sleep between shifts, even though they knew that the creatures of the bog dared not enter the forest with the spirits of the dead protecting it.

In the race to find the cave the evening before, they'd had little time to gauge the size of the forest or any details about it. Enob stuck his head out of the cave and took in the scene around them. The ghosts of the dryads had drifted back into the Land of Shadow when the sun had risen, and there was no sign of any predators looking for an early meal.

The wizard pulled himself back into the cave and took in the little company. "The coast is clear; we shouldn't encounter any trouble as long as we follow the path though this miserable place. It seems that the daylight drives the dead away, and the locals seem too afraid to enter the wood even in the light."

The wizard turned to Kestrel. "The source of the poison will be at the center of the forest. Do you have any idea how big this place is? I would like to get what we need and return to this cave before the sun sets. I for one don't want to be caught outside after nightfall."

Kestrel shrugged. "I can't be sure, but I think that if we keep a good pace, we should make it to the poison tree by midday."

"Good," said Enob. "That should give us enough time to get a branch and return before dark."

No one seemed to object to this plan. Generally speaking, the thought of being surrounded by those ghosts in the woods at night scared the others to the core. Although the cave wasn't their favorite place, so far it had kept them out of harm's way.

Kestrel and Fox took the lead, and one by one they exited the cave. The path they followed meandered through the skeletal forest. All around them stood the rotting trunks of all manner of trees—some straight,

Sidhe

some twisted, some squat, and others tall and slender. Regardless of size or shape, all the trees had one common characteristic: they were dead.

The light was poor as it filtered through thick, heavy moss that draped across the upper branches, which must once have supported a splendid canopy of leaves. For hours they picked their way among the trees, careful not to trip over the gnarled roots.

At just about midday they spotted the tree they sought. It stood nearly half again as tall as the surrounding forest. It was alive...in a fiendish sort of way. The bark was a pale gray, with meandering streaks of black veins tracing across its rough surface. Long, gnarled branches supported a canopy of lifeless brown leaves, streaked through with the same poisonous black veins.

Kestrel and Fox approached the tree first. They could smell the poison that drained from it, spreading toxins into the earth and absorbing what little life existed in the bog.

Enob climbed the hillock and touched the trunk. "This tree is the source of the evil that surrounds us."

He walked around the base of the tree, sliding his hand across the knobby bark and examining every detail. He stopped next to a large hole, where age had rotted away a section of trunk to the core, and looked up into the canopy. "I'll need a long, straight branch."

Fox nodded and withdrew a long dagger from his boot. Using the knothole to gain a foothold, he climbed up the tree to the first section of branches. When he found a suitable bough and began to cut through the bark, he called out to the wizard.

"What about the poison?"

Enob turned and looked up at the young Sentinel. "Not to worry—the poison strips life from the land. It would take considerably longer than this for its taint to affect us." The wizard almost smiled. "Anyway, surrounded by this bog, I'm more concerned about our short-term life expectancy than what our future health has in store for us."

Fox slid back down the tree with a long branch in his hand. "Great! Just what I wanted to hear."

Enob examined the wood and nodded. "This will do nicely. Now let's get back to that cave so that I can make something of it. The clock's ticking!"

The small party took a final look at the tree. They all seemed to feel the poison leaching out into the ground, and no one objected to leaving.

A raven watched as the little group wandered back down the path along which they had come. It might have smiled if it had been able.

Not long before the sun set and the creatures of the bog began to crawl from their dwellings, the company found themselves back in the relative safety of the root cave. The wizard didn't waste a moment. He removed a set of tools from his pack and, with a skilled, delicate hand, began to whittle away at the wood. When satisfied that he had formed the arrow in an acceptable shape, he took great care in sanding the shaft until the black veins of poison were clearly defined in the smooth, gray wood.

The wizard laid out three blood-red feathers that he had brought with him, and he attached them to the back of the arrow shaft. Then with his knife he notched a small slit on the business end of the shaft and inserted a razor-sharp obsidian arrowhead. Finally he carved a series of mysterious sigils into the wood and, in a burst of red light, energized them with a touch of magic.

Satisfied with his creation, he peered into the dark woods outside the mouth of the cave and then turned to his companions. "The arrow has been shaped, but it is not quite finished. I'll need to do this alone."

He pulled his dark cowl over his head and stepped out into the darkness. Both Fox and Kestrel tried to stop him, but the wizard wouldn't be swayed.

"Don't worry…my magic will protect me. This has to be done, and I don't have the strength to protect us all together. This is the only way to ensure that the arrow will work when we need it to."

Fox and Kestrel watched the wizard as he slipped into the darkness. From behind them, Murdox snorted.

"He just loves the drama, doesn't he?"

The two young elves turned to the wolf-dog, shaking their heads in disbelief.

Outside, Enob found a small tree stump that would suit his purpose and placed the arrow on top of it. He listened and waited for what he knew would

Sidhe

come.

When the first of the wailing spirits arrived, he began to whisper and weave his magic into the air. Soon he was surrounded by the ethereal spirits of the dryads. Hatred of the living filled their eyes, but Enob's magic held them at bay. For a short moment he watched them drift through the trees, feeling both sorrow and shame for what they had become. He mingled his magic into the words he spoke.

"The Great Tree has once again risen from the earth. You can already feel it's presence on the land, and its strength will only grow until all else succumbs to its might." He stretched out his arms and pressed his magic deeper into the words. "Of all the creatures of this world, you alone can prevent this, and you alone understand what this means to the world. You are now paying the price for your crimes in life. If there is any compassion left in your souls…do the right thing now."

The wraiths drifted through the trees, held in check only by the powerful wizard's magical energy and will. They cared little for the living, but something deep in the darkness of their souls stirred. They gazed at the wizard in indecision, and Enob felt a chill run down his spine. Was it his magic or the slightest hint of compassion that swayed them? He would never know, but in the end they acquiesced.

One by one they drifted to the arrow and touched it with their vaporous hands, allowing their lethal magic to course through the shaft. Ages ago this touch would have been one of healing; now it meant only death.

Enob returned ashen-faced to the cave. His strength was drained, and he needed rest. The task was a success; he could feel the cursed magic coursing through the arrow. If they could reach the Tree before its roots dug into the soil beneath Cloudview, the arrow would destroy it.

Just as the sun broke free of the horizon, the little company emerged from the cave. Kestrel took the lead and led them back through the dead forest and into the bog. Once again the bog was quiet—there were no signs of life. The nocturnal predators had crawled back into the mud they called home and were waiting for darkness to fall once more, in time for the next hunt.

The same meandering path led them through the maze of dark pools. A few of their tracks still remained where the mud and ooze hadn't covered them over. Almost immediately Kase, Murdox, and Enob were completely lost, but somehow Kestrel and Fox were able to follow what seemed like an invisible path. Without the constant backtracking they had made on their journey here, they now made good time on their return.

Kestrel turned and looked at the weary faces of her friends. "At this pace, we should be free of this vile place by midday."

A muddy brown crest broke the surface of the fetid pool, hardly creating a disturbance in the calm water. Two black eyes watched the small company pass by the pool, and when they had gone, the reptilian creature pulled itself silently out of the stagnant water.

Mostly humanoid in shape, it was approximately six feet tall, standing upright on two legs. Its skin was scaled and colored a greenish-brown.

Both its hands and feet were webbed between the digits, and a long, thin membrane ran down the length of its back in a low crest. It wore no discernable clothing, only metal bands on its wrists and ankles that were adorned with strange markings.

As was their usual routine, Kestrel was at point, followed by Enob, Kase, and Murdox. Fox was taking up the rear. He had realized early on that they were being watched and was certain, from the way she rested her palm on her sword, that Kestrel knew as well. He had decided not to warn the others and to wait and see what happened, hoping they might pass by any danger. Things changed immediately when he sensed the creature pulling itself from the water, and he knew the waiting was over.

The creature had with it a long, barbed spear, which it raised overhead and threw at what it hoped was an easy meal. Years of combat training instantly alerted Fox to the danger, and he whirled in place, pulling his sword from its sheath so quickly that the two movements seemed as one. He swung downward with the razor-sharp elven blade, easily slicing through the wood shaft of the spear and cleaving it in half.

The adjacent pools burbled and boiled as many more of the strange troglodyte creatures pulled themselves free of the water. They soon surrounded the party, brandishing spears and metal nets.

Instinctively the fellowship tightened their group so that each covered the other's back just as the creatures charged forward, brandishing their spears. Enob was a moment faster than the others, using his magic to create a protective sphere that surrounded the party. Still weakened from the extreme exertion the evening before, his conjuring was only enough for their first strike—but that was all Fox and Kestrel needed.

The two younger elves were on the move. They met the attack head on, clashing offensively, steel on steel with the attackers. In a whirlwind of spins and twists, they each downed three of the foes. In just a matter of moments, they had reduced the enemy by half, but a few managed to slip through the maelstrom of swinging blades.

Murdox butted Kase in the leg. "Well, shoot them already!"

Mesmerized by the suddenness of the battle, Kase barely had time to pull his weapon from the holster and get off a shot from his Berrington Model 13 pistol before the attackers could reach them. The energy beam pulsed from the gun, blasting into one of the creatures at the shoulder, spinning him around, and knocking him to the ground. Murdox leapt at a second one and slammed it backwards into the mud. Kase quickly took advantage of the situation and got off another shot from his pistol, firing it pointblank into the chest of the fallen troglodyte. Electrostatic energy pulsated around the beast in waves of blue light, instantly overloading the creature's neural system and knocking it unconscious.

Too busy to notice everything going on, the group didn't see a third creature sneak up behind them and throw a metal net over Murdox. With the wolf-dog momentarily preoccupied with the netting, the reptilian assailant then grabbed Kase and knocked him to the ground.

Kestrel was in the midst of an attack against two enemies when she saw Kase hit the ground, but at that moment she was having her own problems. Fortunately for Kase, one of her attackers made a critical mistake and thrust his spear farther than he should have. The elf scout faded to the side as the barbed shaft slid past her, and she grabbed it with her free hand, bracing it between her arm and body. Using the energy of the creature's attack, she transformed the forward thrust of the spear into a circular motion by rotating her hips at the same time. The beast, still hanging onto the spear tightly, found itself completely off balance and slammed into the second of her attackers. With Kase on the ground, she knew she had precious little time to waste and quickly finished them off.

Fox spotted Enob struggling with one of the beasts. Three of the creatures lay fallen around him, and it was obvious that the wizard was near exhaustion. His magic seemed to be fading, and he needed help. In one bound, Fox leapt into the air and, with a perfectly executed kick, crushed what he presumed was the ribcage of the last of his own adversaries. Before he even hit the ground, the young Sentinel had a dagger in hand and hurtled it at the beast that was fighting Enob.

One Wizard Place

Kase landed face-first in the mud, losing his gun in the fall. He fumbled in the muck to reach the weapon, but he only managed to lose his grip on the slippery handle. Before he could get a good hold on the gun, a troglodyte was on top of him. They wrestled for a moment, but the beast was far stronger than the young agent. The creature pinned Kase to the ground and raised a dagger over his head.

Kase forced his eyes shut and figured that he was about to meet his maker, but just as the killing blow should have fallen, he heard a *thump* directly beside him. He waited a moment longer before opening his eyes. There, lying next to him, was the monster, facedown in the mud with a long, white arrow protruding from its back.

In the turmoil one of the troglodytes grabbed the net that bound Murdox and dragged it to the edge of the pool. The wolf-dog struggled against the metal netting, but he couldn't get himself free before the creature dragged him into the filthy water. Desperately Murdox tried to keep his head above the water, but the beast was too strong, and the wolf-dog slipped below the surface. Fox leapt into the water after him while Kestrel and Enob finished off the rest of the troglodytes, driving them back into the surrounding pools to nurse their wounds.

More than a minute passed after Fox followed Murdox into the pool, and still there was no sign of either of them. Kase and Kestrel were just about to jump in after them when bubbles rose to the surface. A moment later, a very irritated wolf-dog emerged from the depths, spitting foul water all around him. Then Fox hit the surface, inhaling a huge lungful of air.

Back on land, Murdox coughed up more of the filthy liquid and spat it back into the pool.

"It's a good thing he's got such a big mouth," said Kase.

"Why's that?" Kestrel asked.

Kase and Enob smiled and said in unison, "Plenty of hot air!"

-Chapter Ten-

Watchers

Gliding on the rising air currents that drifted up from the mountain, the raven watched as the small party crossed out of the bog. Satisfied that all was the way it should be, it allowed the wind to carry it upward until it cleared the top of one of the lower peaks.

It was just after dusk when the little company found their owls waiting for them in the foothills just beyond the rock outcropping that extended into the bog. They were a welcome site indeed after two horrendous days in such a dreadful place.

After a short hike into the hills to find a safer place to sleep, they decided that it wasn't worth going any farther that night. Exhausted, they opted to make camp in a hollow near the base of the mountain and get an early start the next morning. They set up a makeshift base and cooked their first warm meal in days.

Not long after the plates were cleared, each of them dove into a bedroll and fell asleep under the stars. That night they didn't post a watch, confident that their birds would wake them at the first sign of trouble.

They awoke early the next morning to a miserable day. A layer of dense fog clung to the ground, saturating their clothes and making visibility nearly impossible. After trying numerous times to keep a fire going, they finally gave up and ate a cold breakfast.

Kestrel poked at the wet logs with a stick and spoke to the group.

"To reach Myrr Wood from here, we'll have to fly for about three days. This part of the country is fairly safe, and I doubt we'll run into too much trouble until we get closer to the Sídhe kingdom. I realize it's been a tough couple of days, but for at least a little while we might be able to relax a bit."

Kase grabbed a towel from his pack and rubbed his wet hair with it.

"Tell me about Myrr Wood," he asked Kestrel

as he passed her the towel. "What does it have in store for us?"

Kestrel patted her damp face, then went on. "The forest is huge—days upon days of travel from one side to the other. It's a gloomy place with hanging moss and strangled trees. Danger is all about, the air hangs thick like oil, and in the dim light everything is in shades of green and black. Occasionally a stray beam of sunlight slips through the tangled boughs, but those are rare moments of illumination, and as you go deeper, they lessen and soon cease altogether. It's eerily silent in those woods, and the trees are always watching, closing in all around you until you feel like a small, insignificant speck that could be crushed at any moment. No…I'd say it's not a very nice place to visit, and to make matters worse, we're not welcome there."

For many long moments, they were all silent.

"Why do these trips always have to be so lousy?" the irritable wolf-dog finally said. "All I want to do is take a little trip to the beach—maybe do some sailing and work on a tan."

Kase scratched him behind the ears to calm him

down. "You know you can't get a tan...you're covered in fur."

Murdox thumped his paw on the ground. "Whatever. You get my point."

Enob stood up. "Friends, this is where I must say ado. As you know, I won't be joining you for the trek into the forest. I need to get back to the city to help Commander Crashblade keep the peace. My magic will be more useful to slow the roots' progress as they make their way toward the ground. We need to buy as much time as possible for you to get to the Tree and end this."

An hour later they had broken camp and saddled the owls. Kestrel and Fox double-checked the rigs, making sure the equipment was properly stowed and cushioned for silent flight. Each of the young elves was greatly impressed with the other's skills and knowledge, and both felt comforted finally to have found a companion so similar in age and in natural talents and abilities and training.

After taking a heading from her map and making sure the others were settled and ready, Kestrel pulled herself into her saddle, with Kase seated behind her, and tightened the safety harness around her waist. The elf scout then turned her bird so that she could see Fox and Murdox.

"We'll fly northwest until noon and break for a light lunch. I don't expect much trouble, but to be safe, let's keep low and stay to the forest whenever we can."

After they had all said their final farewells to Enob, the birds leapt silently from the ground and instantly disappeared from view as the mist swallowed them in its folds.

By late morning of the third day after leaving the bog, Kestrel spun her bird in a tight circle around a small clearing surrounded by tall oaks. Satisfied that there were no unwanted guests in their latest landing zone, she waved the others in. This had been their routine for the last leg of the journey, and she hoped their luck would hold. She had other plans in mind and wanted them to be safe without her for a short while. The journey had been relatively easy, and by using the owls' near-perfect night vision, they were able to fly well into the evening and make up some much needed time. Thankfully, they had encountered little trouble in the last few days, but with Myrr Wood so close, she knew that was about to change.

The elf scout hopped from her saddle and scratched her great gray owl on the side of its head as she helped Kase from his seat. "The edge of Myrr Wood is only a couple of hour's flight from here," she told the others. "I want to scout up ahead and see what we have in store for us."

She waited for Fox to object, but the wise young Sentinel nodded approval. He realized that Kestrel knew the Park better than anyone, and with danger so close, they couldn't afford to run into any unexpected surprises.

"We made good time in the last few days. I think it's a smart idea for us to grab a bite to eat and recover some strength." Fox patted Murdox on the head and assured Kestrel, "I'll look after these guys while you're gone. See if you can find safe passage into the forest and make our lives a little easier."

Murdox almost smiled.

Kestrel gave her bird a few minutes to rest before hopping back into the saddle. "It shouldn't take too long to scout the area. If all goes well, I'll be back before the sun sets."

Fox acted as though he were tightening down one of the straps on her saddle so they could talk softly. With Kase and Murdox out of earshot, he asked, "What do you sense?"

Kestrel shook her head. "I really don't know. I don't have a very good feeling about this, but I haven't been able to pinpoint anything. Something in the air…it just doesn't feel right."

Fox nodded. "I feel it, as well, but we don't have much of a choice, do we?"

Kestrel shrugged. "Let's just hope we're both wrong. Hopefully I'll find us a safe route that will let us slip into the forest with as little resistance as possible…but I'm not very optimistic."

Fox pondered her words for a minute, then said, "Just be careful. I don't want to finish this alone."

She smiled and lightly jabbed her heels into the bird's ribs.

Sidhe

The young Sentinel watched her take off in a cloud of dust and disappear from sight.

On silent wings, the elf scout flew her bird only inches over the treetops. She was glad that a light morning fog still clung to the ground and trees, as it gave her a measure of protection from being spotted. Staying low within the mist, she flew the bird right up to a cliff, landing in a small clearing about fifty yards from the edge.

She climbed down from the saddle and whispered into her owl's ear. "Stay hidden. I'll be back as soon as I can. Keep a listen for my call; I may need your help before this is over."

The big bird blinked, seeming aloof, but Kestrel knew better. She and this bird had flown together for years, and she trusted him completely. He would not readily abandon her.

Not forgetting for a minute what had happened to her the last time she was here, the elf paid particular attention to her surroundings. She allowed herself a moment of quiet and extended her senses for as far as she could. Danger was near, but for the moment she and the bird were safe from watchful eyes.

Carefully she made her way to the edge of the cliff and peered into the valley. The forest was as it has always been: dark and dangerous, an unending tangle of gnarled and twisted trees. Within that fearful wall of wood was where they needed to go, for in that dreadful place lay the Sídhe kingdom…and the Faerie Queen.

This time, however, the army that had stood guard was gone. Not a soul could be found as far as she could see, although evidence of its presence remained. The ground had been trampled into submission, pocked with blackened fire pits, and littered with the refuse that always accompanies men and beasts.

The hair on the back of her neck prickled, and she had the uncomfortable feeling that she was not alone. Peering down, she scanned the cliff wall for sentries, but after a thorough search she could find no sign of their presence. Unable to shrug off her concern completely, she slipped into a fissure in the wall that ran down the side of the cliff. Confident that she could stay concealed within the crevice, the elf silently climbed down to the ground below.

There remained the matter of crossing the gap between the cliff and the forest. There she would be exposed to anyone watching from above; but after studying the terrain and discarding a number of possibilities, she thought that she could discern a suitable route and picked a path that she felt should keep her unseen for most of the trek.

The green-skinned fae scanned the valley below. Days had passed since the army of vile beasts had moved on. Called by the Queen, they were commanded to move inward and tighten the circle, getting ever closer to the growing Tree. For days no sign of life had appeared in the small rift. The army had cleaned out the surrounding forest of game in an attempt to quench their never-sated hunger. Any remaining animals had fled the area or were too afraid of the forest to get any closer. True to his task, though, he remained vigilant, watching for anything that might pass. His Queen would expect nothing less.

One Wizard Place

Kestrel pulled her concealing cloak from her pack and drew the hood over her head. With great stealth she slowly threaded herself through a chain of boulders that had broken away from the cliff and scattered across the field. Inch by inch she made her way over the rough terrain. Through patience, skill, and the camouflaging qualities of her concealing cloak, she managed to mimic the surrounding rocks and foliage and was able to cross the boulder slide safely, nearly to the edge of the forest.

Her hopes died away when she reached the end of the debris and realized that the army's encampment had destroyed any vegetation that might have provided protection from watchful eyes. Certain that she was still concealed by the rubble, she rolled onto her back to get a better look at the cliff. For many long moments she peered up at the wall, but as before she couldn't see any lookouts. Still that nagging feeling persisted and kept her from dashing across the last stretch.

Just as she was finally about to gather herself up and run, she spotted the tiniest motion about three quarters up the rock wall. There he was, hidden in a small cleft that had been obscured by natural vegetation and the angle of the wall. Only his slight movement had given him away; if he had stayed still a second longer, she would have given up her hiding place and surely been spotted.

From her vantage she could see him, although she was sure he hadn't spotted her. Yet there was still the matter of crossing the remnants of the encampment without being seen.

As she pondered what to do next, an unlikely answer flew overhead. A raven glided in over the top of the cliff and began circling a piece of ground a good distance away from where she was. Kestrel kept her eye on the faerie sentry as he poked his head out from his hiding spot, watching the raven's antics. Whatever the bird was doing, it had taken the sentry's attention away from the valley below.

The bird started to tighten it circle and cawed more frequently, focusing its attention on the ground. It weaved up and down for a moment, and Kestrel knew it was about to dive. This was the chance she needed. She waited for the exact moment the bird began its descent, and the moment it did, she was up and running. By the time the bird returned to the sky and began circling once more, she was already concealed deep within the trees of Myrr Wood.

−Chapter Eleven−
Faerie Dust in the Morning

The day was growing long. Kestrel had been gone for more than seven hours, but Fox wasn't worried.

The young Sentinel was trained in countless fighting styles, stealth, military tactics, philosophical reasoning, and more languages than most people would hear in a lifetime. He could hide in plain sight, travel over a sandy beach and not leave a trackable footprint and, if the need arose, fight like a cornered dragon.

Few in the world could match his skill…save Kestrel. From the moment he'd met her, he was convinced that he had met his equal. If anyone could return from a hopeless situation, she could, and thus he wasn't worried…much.

"I need a snack!"

Murdox snuffled around the campsite, foraging

through their travel packs for something to eat.

"All this waiting around makes me hungry."

Kase gave him a stern glance. "Just quiet down. We'll eat in a couple of hours. Maybe Kestrel will return by then."

"But I'm hungry now," said the wolf-dog.

Kase waved a hand in the direction of his supplies. "Fine. I think there are some candy bars in my pack. Just save a few for the rest of us."

Murdox had hardly heard a word of the last sentence. He was already up to his shoulders in the boy's magical backpack.

The wolf-dog emerged with what was left of the chocolate bar he'd found. "This whole thing is getting worse by the minute," he complained to Kase. "If what Kestrel says is true, we're going to have a heck of a time slipping through an army of all-magicked-up monsters. Both of us know that we couldn't very well be called world-class fighters, and I doubt we could sneak through a camp of deaf and blind trolls that were half asleep without getting caught."

Kase really didn't have much to say after that.

Sidhe

For the most part, he really couldn't disagree with what Murdox had said...and this wasn't exactly their cup of tea.

"But the good news is that I found an extra steak in here. If we're going down, I want it to be on a full stomach," said the wolf-dog.

Both Fox and Kase just shrugged, pulled up a log, and started a fire.

Kestrel followed the footprints for more than an hour, yet she couldn't find any sign that she was getting closer to the army. Frustrated, she continued deeper into the woods, but with every step she took, her apprehension grew. More and more she had the eerie feeling that someone was watching her. From the moment the elf had entered Myrr Wood, she'd known she wasn't wanted there, but until now it had only been a generalized feeling. Now it was becoming focused.

After another few minutes, her agitation peaked, and the hair rose on the back of her neck. The elf scout grabbed hold of her dagger and slipped into the crook of a tree. She quieted her mind and reached out with her senses. Danger surrounded her, then suddenly it was everywhere at one time. It bombarded her senses in a rush of white noise that knocked her backwards into the tree. Horrified by the incident, she dropped her dagger and slipped down to the base of the trunk, shaking like a leaf. Never had she felt so much rage at one time.

She grabbed both of her knees and pulled herself into a ball. For the next few minutes, all she could do was breath. It took everything she had to drive the fear back down and regain control. This mission was far too important to panic; they all were depending on her to find passage through this forest and reach the Tree in time to end this quest with success.

She took a couple of minutes more to gather her strength and resolved herself to go on. Then she picked up her dagger and stood. She stepped away from the tree and walked carefully back to the trail of footprints, one step at a time, until she had her senses back. Everything around her seemed to be her enemy, and she couldn't shake the feeling that she was being watched, but she moved on nonetheless.

Sidhe

High up in the branches, the imp watched. It swished its thin tail back and forth as it peered into the woods below. Brainwashed by the Faerie Queen, the imp resisted its natural urge to cause mischief and mayhem and instead sat still, scanning the woods for trespassers.

The small red devil was pondering its misery when it heard a branch crunch below. The beast tensed and focused on the forest floor... and there, not fifty feet below, was an elf.

The little fiend pulled a long, saw-toothed dagger from a sling it wore on its shoulder and took aim at the girl.

"Silly elf, tricks are for pixies."

Just as it was about to throw the weapon, a raven flew across its path and broke its concentration. The feathers on the bird rippled, and its outline blurred. A second later the bird resolved into a little green-skinned man, hardly bigger than the imp. The last thing the beast saw was the sight of its own dagger twisting around in the air, followed by utter darkness.

"And daggers are for demons," said the little

faerie as it jumped from the branch, and glistening black feathers sprouted again across its body.

With an audible thump, the body of a red imp fell from the sky and landed in a heap only a few feet in front of Kestrel. The elf nudged the diminutive sprite with her toe, but the creature didn't stir. Before she had a chance to ponder this any further, a black raven landed on top of the dagger that was sticking out of the little fiend's chest. Content to roost on this perch, it ruffled its feathers and faced the elf girl. In its yellow beak it held a small, rolled-up scroll, which it dropped at Kestrel's feet.

The bird suddenly turned its head to the forest behind it and cawed, but Kestrel already knew something was seriously wrong. She grabbed the scroll, jammed it into her belt, and took off running.

The forest behind the elf exploded. The trees swayed and groped, waving one way and another without any wind to blow them around. Branches snapped, and the trunks uprooted, tearing away from the ground and falling directly in her wake. She turned and saw a monstrous wave of green and brown chasing after her. The forest behind her was collapsing like a row of dominos falling one after the other. The sound was deafening, like a hurricane slamming into a costal town and tearing down everything in its path. Mixed into the noise were also voices—harsh, scrambled voices screaming at her, driving her back to the boundary of the woods.

Kestrel ran flat out for as long as she could. Dirt and debris sprayed her back, and leaves rushed toward her face. She waved her arms in front of her as if trying to swim through the foliage that flew past and cut her as it went by. Somehow she managed to stay a few feet ahead of the maelstrom.

She couldn't tell if hours or only minutes had passed, but she felt that her heart was going to rip from her chest. Finally completely spent, she could go on no longer and fell to the forest floor. She lay flat on her back, looking up at the canopy far above, and her heart pounded under her ribcage as she gasped for air, trying to catch her breath.

When she finally recovered enough to look in

the direction from which she had just come, she couldn't believe her eyes. Nothing was amiss. The forest was quiet, and only a light breeze rustled through the leaves. The voices had ceased, and the trees stood upright as they should. It was as if nothing had happened at all. For as far as she could see, the woods were as they had appeared on her way in: dark and foreboding, still watching and mocking her, but no different than before.

She wanted nothing more than to be rid of this place…but it wasn't over yet. Far in the distance, she heard the howling of hungry dogs. The elf was on the move again and quickened her pace back to a sprint. There was a glow ahead, still dim. Maybe she could reach the end of the woods before the vile beasts could catch up with her. As she closed in on the light ahead, the whining and baying seemed much closer. Then it was coming from all around her.

The dogs were close, so very close. They could smell her sweat and sense her fear. In a frenzy they raced toward their prey. Hunger kept them going. They were always kept hungry, continually starved by their cruel masters. This way, when they needed to hunt, they would be desperate to make the catch. Food was near, and they could almost taste their next meal. Closer, ever closer they drew as they closed in on their quarry. Close…so very close.

The woods crashed apart, and she was surrounded by the wild eyes of the hunting dogs. Faced with a life-or-death situation, Kestrel pulled out her sword, and the beasts attacked from all directions. The pack clawed and bit at her, but she kept them at bay, taking down one, two, three of the creatures until she had cleared a path in front of her. She took off at a run, winding through the trees and fighting off the hounds when they came too close. She made a dash for the boundary of the forest, pulling her whistle from around her neck as she ran and blowing into it as hard as she dared.

Finally she broke free of the forest, only to be greeted by a small party of ogres smiling devilishly at her. She had fallen into their trap like a scared rabbit. They laughed at the young scout, lowering their pikes and spears in an attempt to impale the girl as she almost ran into them.

The devil dogs were right behind her. Thinking fast, she took advantage of the situation. She leapt to a boulder and used her speed to propel herself into the air, flying over the heads of the ogres in a single bound. The dogs couldn't stop in time and instead found the business ends of the ogres' weapons.

On silent wings Kestrel's owl glided over the treetops of Myrr Wood and dove into the clearing. It opened its talons and raked them across the ogres, dropping a few of them to the ground. The great owl turned in the air and slowed as it got closer to Kestrel. As the bird flew by, she leaped into the air, grabbed her saddled, and pulled herself into the seat. She had just gotten situated when she caught movement on the rock cliff in front of her.

Two gray-green dracon-flies lifted from their perches in some hidden fold in the rock wall. They each carried an armored rider who was currently aiming a longbow in her direction. Kestrel pulled hard left on her flight reins and veered away from the riders, steering her owl back to the forest. She brought the owl into the trees, finding a path that allowed it to navigate between the tightly spaced trunks. For its size it was remarkably agile and naturally adept at flying in close spaces under the canopy of a forest, but this was still an extremely difficult task.

With a thwack, two arrows cracked into the trees, far too close for Kestrel's comfort. Her owl was flying as fast as it could, but the dracon-flies took up chase and dove into the forest in pursuit of Kestrel and her mount.

The bird weaved between the countless old trees, deftly cutting left and right, soaring up and down and around the maze of branches and trunks as it tried to lose its pursuers. Even more agile than the owl, the dracon-flies closed the gap. They were built to fly in the woods; their four wings and slender bodies gave them the ability to rip through turns and accelerate with blinding speed.

Kestrel flew her bird left and right, up and over the bows of the trees, a hair's breathe from disaster every second. Arrows whistled by her head, close enough that she could feel the pressure wave as they slammed into one tree after another. She flew her bird as close to the ground as she dared, banking the creature into a nearly impossible turn as an arrow slipped through the tip of the bird's outermost feathers.

The dracon-flies flanked her, and their fae riders took careful aim; but the instant they released their bow strings, Kestrel pulled herself from her saddle and let the bird fly out from underneath her. The arrows whooshed by her, passing only inches from her body as she fell to the ground. She hit hard, rolling backwards to dissipate the energy of the fall. The next moment she was on her feet with a longbow in her hand and an arrow nocked into the string. She drew back the bow and released the missile at her target. It tore through the air, ripping a long gash in the thin membrane of one of the four wings of the closest dracon-fly. The beast veered hard as it howled in pain, missing a necessary maneuver, and then it clipped a second wing on a tree, which sent it to the ground.

Kestrel took the moment to take aim at the second rider, but it was already too late. The dracon-fly was nearly on top of her, and she was forced to drop to her belly as it sailed just over her head. The creature turned back and tried a second time, but Kestrel had already moved out of the way.

The fae rider cruised in low, heading to where the elf had been a moment before. He was clearly upset: somehow this creature had eluded all of his efforts to eliminate her. Now she had disappeared. One moment she was prone on her belly, and the next she was gone. The green-skinned fae slowed his mount as he searched the surrounding woods for the trespasser, but she was nowhere to be seen.

Kestrel had seized the moment when the dracon-fly had turned to slip behind a tree, using her concealing cloak to keep her temporarily hidden in the dim light. When the dracon passed by her tree, she jumped out from her hiding spot and grabbed onto the creature's saddle, flinging herself around and slamming into the rider head on. For a moment the two struggled, kicking and punching one another, but Kestrel was by far the superior fighter, and she had him out of the saddle and facedown on the forest floor in no time.

The elf took hold of the dracon-fly's reins and pointed the creature back to the boundary of the forest while whistling for her owl. The bird appeared a moment later, pursued by no less than five more of the mounted dracon-flies.

Her owl matched speed with the dracon-fly she was on, and the elf jumped back onto her bird. She let the owl accelerate just above the forest floor, using the ground affect to gather speed. When she spied an opening in the canopy far above, she pointed the bird to the sky. They broke free of the trees moments before the dracon-flies could catch up with them.

The elf pulled the bird into a series of evasive maneuvers as the fae pursuer fired arrow after arrow at her. She did her best to avoid the hail of fire, but one of the razor-sharp blades struck her in the leg, only to be stopped by her armor before it did any serious damage. Kestrel continued to push her bird skyward as its massive lungs pumped fresh oxygen into its bloodstream, allowing the bird to climb ever higher into the clouds. Soon they had outpaced their pursers, and the arrows began to fall away harmlessly behind.

-Chapter Twelve-

Horror Stories

Kestrel dragged herself into the campsite much later that evening. Fox was waiting for her to return, but he held his tongue so that she might sit and compose herself before he asked any questions.

The young Sentinel walked up behind the elf scout and put his hand on her shoulder. She looked up, perplexed, but Fox just smiled and yanked out an arrow that was lodged in her shoulder armor.

"Yow! Where'd that come from?" the elf girl exclaimed.

She took the arrow from Fox and examined a small drop of blood on the tip. "I knew I had one in my leg, which I pulled out earlier, but I had no idea that was there. Anything else back there that I should know about?"

Fox shook his head. "Nope. That was it...but you can thank that good armor of yours. You hardly got more than a scratch."

Kestrel examined the finely crafted blade of the arrow and couldn't disagree.

"So tell me about it," said Fox.

Kestrel shook her head and begged off. "There are only a few hours until daylight. How about you let me get some sleep, and we'll talk in the morning?"

"Fair enough. I'll see you then," said Fox as he strolled to the edge of the fire's glow and took up watch.

Despite all Fox's own special qualities and discipline, Kestrel never ceased to amaze the Sentinel. Just knowing that he was keeping her and the others safer made the time on watch go more quickly and made it seem less like drudgery to stay awake and alert.

The next morning came far too quickly for Kestrel. She groaned and stretched her sore muscles, wincing from the pain of far too many cuts and scratches. She looked across the campsite and saw Fox stoking the fire below a pot of boiling water, and she staggered over to warm her hands.

The sun had only been up for a short while, and the light was just beginning to penetrate the deep forest, illuminating the fog around them. Murdox scuffled around the woods for a few minutes and then trotted into the camp when he heard Kestrel's voice.

The wolf-dog nuzzled her in the leg. "Well look what the cat dragged in. You look like you lost a fight with a troll."

Kestrel groaned. "Worse…."

Kase came up beside her and patted her on the shoulder, causing her to flinch.

"Sorry about that. How are you this morning?"

Kestrel gave them all a weary look while Fox stirred some tea leaves into the boiling water. "Kase, grab a few mugs, and we'll have some tea while we listen to what should be an interesting story," he said.

Kestrel blew into her tea and took a long sip before telling them what had happened.

"I flew as close to Myrr Wood as I dared. Then

I crept to the edge of the cliff and peered into the valley below...but the army was gone." The elf rubbed a sore shoulder muscle and continued. "I was determined to find out what was going on, so I snuck across the valley and followed the army's tracks into the woods. From the moment I entered, I felt something was terribly wrong. I followed the tracks for as long as I dared, but the faeries had stationed a lookout in the trees. That's when all the fun began. The lookout was a little red imp who decided to shoot first and ask questions later. If it weren't for our bird friend, I might not be talking with you now."

The elf pulled the tightly wound scroll from her belt and handed it to Fox. "The raven's generosity didn't end there," she continued. "He dumped that scroll at my feet. Before I had a chance to look it over, though, everything broke loose." Kestrel hesitated and tried to gather her thoughts. "I have never been so terrified in my life. The woods came alive. It's really hard to explain, but suffice it to say that the forest came down around me and, literally in a wave of destruction, chased me until I didn't have the stamina to run any longer. I ran flat out for as long as I ever have in my life and was only able to stay a step ahead of instant death. When I couldn't go any farther, I just collapsed to the ground…and for a moment there, I thought I had bought the farm."

She shook her head in frustration and then suddenly smiled before going on.

"But when I looked up, the forest was back to normal…except of course for the Thraken hunting dogs, the Scarpothian ridgebacks, a few demon-jackals, and the ogres that controlled them. They had me trapped like a rat—and before I realized it, I was ambushed. If not for my owl, I would have been in serious trouble. Oh, wait…I *was* in serious trouble! As soon as I thought I had made it out alive, the faeries attacked me on their dracon-flies."

Kestrel rubbed her thigh gingerly where she had been shot with an arrow just the day before. "After some trouble I defeated two of them, only to be attacked by at least five more. With a little fancy flying, I was finally able to evade them and make it out of the forest into clear air. I made sure I wasn't followed and then flew directly here—a little worse for wear, but alive nonetheless."

Murdox sat back on his haunches. "Well, that sounds easy enough.... Phew! I was a little worried that we might have some problems on our hands."

"Quiet," said Kase.

Fox had been standing there with the pot of steaming tea in his hand, mesmerized by Kestrel's tale. "I agree with Murdox. Sounds like a piece of cake. When do we get started?"

They all looked at him in amazement.

"What? I was only kidding...just trying to lighten the mood," said Fox, looking a bit sheepish after his first failed attempt at humor. The young Sentinel unfurled the scroll and rolled it out on a flat rock so they could all see.

Kestrel traced her fingers across the paper and said with a grimace, "It's a map...and from what I can glean, we're *here,* and we want to be *here*."

Fox followed her finger and groaned. "I think we had better re-think the way through the woods."

The elf scout's shoulders slumped. "Normally I

would agree, but in this case we just can't—we'd never make it that way." She tapped her finger on a strange symbol on the map. "We're going to have to go this way."

Kase and Murdox had no idea what they were talking about.

"Well, what is that spot that's got the two of you so worked up?" asked Murdox.

Kestrel looked at Kase and the wolf-dog for a long moment. "If we can't go through the forest, then we're just going to have to go under it. From what this map says, there's a tunnel that leads from this spot to what looks like the Faerie Queen's doorstep."

Murdox brightened. "That doesn't sound so bad. I can handle being underground, and neither Kase or I are claustrophobic."

Kestrel raised her eyebrows. "One of the problems is that this tunnel is actually a prison—and where faeries are concerned, caves are never a good thing. You see, they love nature and the open air. They can only be happy with the sun on their faces and wind in their hair. They need crystal clear waters and deep woods to survive, and they despise caves. To a faerie, being trapped in a cave is the greatest punishment of them all. If they are actually imprisoned in these tunnels, they would have to be the worst kinds of criminals."

"Well doesn't that just sound like a regular tunnel of love?" muttered Murdox.

Kase looked at Kestrel. "You said 'one of the problems.' What's the other?"

Kestrel nodded to Fox, who said, "You see, Kase, the entrance to the tunnel is located in the Tooth Faerie's house."

Murdox's eyes opened wide, and his head sank to the ground. "Oh, I see what you mean."

Kase looked at them all in disbelief. "Wow! The Tooth Faerie is *real,* and she lives here in this world? How cool is *that*! So what's the problem?"

Kestrel, Fox, and Murdox looked at the boy as if he had two heads, and Fox said, "I don't have a clue which Tooth Faerie you're thinking about, but the one that lives here scares us all to pieces."

Kase looked to Kestrel in disbelief as he

gestured toward Fox. "We're talking about the same guy that battled an evil black dragon and won, a guy that in hand-to-hand combat defeated a Nargoyle that scared the phooey out of both Murdox and me, and he did this all without breaking a sweat. This guy is freaked out by the Tooth Faerie!"

Fox grimaced. "Yup...yes, I am."

"So am I," said Kestrel and Murdox almost in unison.

Murdox scratched at the ground with his paw. "You see, here in this world the Tooth Faerie has gone way past having a tooth fetish. She's a nut case, a psycho, a crackpot, a loony bird, and she's got way too many screws loose. Every dictionary is this world could have her picture next to the word *wacko*—she really freaks everyone out."

Fox scratched the wolf-dog behind the ears and looked over at Kestrel. "We're going to have to make a deal with her to get into the tunnel, and we're going to have to do it soon, before it's too late. How far is it to her house?"

Kestrel studied the map for a few seconds. "The

good thing is that it's only about a five hour flight from here."

In an hour they had broken camp and had their packs and riding gear ready to go. Less than ten minutes later, they were flying to the northwest, high over the treetops with the wind to their backs. From their vantage they could see the edge of Myrr Wood stretching out to the horizon, a vast swath of impossible green. It looked harmless from above, but they knew well enough that it was mystical and deadly within.

By early morning the fog had burned off, but a slight chill hung in the air. Kase pulled his cloak tight around himself and settled back in his saddle. The last few days had been long, and the gentle rhythm of the bird's wings soon lulled him to sleep.

He woke to a slight turbulence in the air. Groaning, he peered into the distance and saw a chain of mountains rising up from the ground and running northward in a long, serpentine line as far as he could see.

Kestrel turned when she heard him wake. "Glad

to see that you're still with us. We're just crossing a range of mountains that marks the farthest northwestern boundary of the faerie kingdom. From here it's about a two-day hike due east to the Faerie Queen's castle."

Something caught Kestrel's eye, and she gestured to Fox with a series of hand signals. He nodded, and they steered the owls between two mountain peaks so they were just out of view from the forest.

Kase was watching the rock walls as they flew slightly below the rim of the mountain. "Why not just fly straight to the castle from here?"

Kestrel pulled on the bird's flight reins, and they soared upward just over the edge of the ridgeline so that Kase could see the forest.

The elf pointed to a series of dots just off the horizon. "Because of them…that's why."

"Because of what?" Kase asked.

Kestrel turned and brought the bird back just below the rim of the mountain. "Sorry. I forget that you can't see as well as Fox and I. Those little dots are dragons, and if I can see them from here, they're really big ones. Dragon's aren't very easy to control, and if the Queen has them under her spell, we have no hope of flying anywhere close to the forest, let alone her castle.

They flew like that for the rest of the morning until Fox spotted a thin wisp of smoke drifting up from a small valley between two towering mountain peaks.

Kase pointed toward the smoke. "I'm guessing that's where we're going."

"Yup," said Kestrel.

The birds put down in a grassy field, and as soon as they landed, Fox started to pull off their packs. He dumped a load of gear on the ground and looked over at his companions.

"We need to unpack our gear and figure out exactly what we'll need for the next few days or so. I'm guessing it will be about a two-day hike through the mountain and, if we're extremely lucky, only a couple of days back."

Murdox growled. "Assuming we finish what we started."

"Yes, that's assuming we end this," said Fox. "From the looks of those dragons patrolling the skies, there's no way we can fly over the forest, and from what we heard about Myrr Wood, itself, there's no way of going through it. So, it looks like our only course of action is to go under it."

Kestrel agreed. "Let's pack what we can easily carry on our backs. We need to keep it light. The dregs of the Faerie society are bad enough, but who knows what else we'll be running into on this stage of our adventure."

They unloaded all the gear they needed and packed it into various light packs, which they put on their backs. Fox loaded what they didn't need back into their flight gear and patted the birds on the beaks. He and Kestrel whispered into their ears and stroked them just above where their wings attached to their shoulders.

Kase rubbed his hand over his owl's wing. "What did you tell them?"

Kestrel frowned. "We told them that we should only be gone for a few days. If we don't come back within a week, they can return home."

Not hesitating any longer, Kestrel signaled to

both owls, and they took off in a wake of grass and dirt.

Murdox watched them fly out of sight and groaned. "Great! Deranged gangster fae folk, a nutcase Tooth Faerie, and we just let our only means of transport fly away. Sounds like this is going to be a wonderful week."

They crossed a field of beautiful wildflowers to reach a small cottage that they had seen on their way in. From the outside, the house looked pleasant enough. It faced the grassy valley, and two smaller wings ran back into the lower slopes of the mountains. The walls were constructed of river stone, and the tan roof was thatched, with a small rock chimney that had wisps of white smoke coming out of it.

There was a low picket fence surrounding a manicured courtyard and a tiny path lined with neatly trimmed hedges. The path led directly to the front door of the cottage, and it just happened to be standing wide open.

"I was thinking," said Murdox, "if the Tooth Faerie lets us pass, how are we going to find our way through the tunnels?"

Kestrel kicked at a stone. "The map the bird gave me has a rough outline, but I was hoping the Tooth Faerie might have a better one. If not, we'll just have to make do with what we've got."

Murdox whimpered. "Oh, I see…we have this well planned out."

Kase gave him a seriously dirty look. "Exactly when did we have a chance to figure out a better way?"

Murdox closed his snout and dropped his tail between his legs.

The black raven landed on the thatched roof of the cottage and watched with genuine concern as the little group stepped onto the path leading to the front door.

-Chapter Thirteen-
Tooth Faerie

Commander Devin Crashblade and the elf wizard Enob stood at the edge of a public parking deck and watched as the river of aerial traffic sped by them. The city ceiling high above their heads glimmered with stars. If it weren't for the giant crack running across its magical surface, it would have mimicked the evening sky perfectly. However, it wasn't so much the crack that disturbed them, but rather the long, brown root that hung from the breach and quickly grew downward.

Enob raised his hand over his head and pointed it in the direction of the root. A blue glow formed in his palm, and a blast of magic shot out like lightening, jacketing the root in static energy. The root burned from the wave of magic and then fell away from the crack in the false sky, landing in a smoldering heap at their feet.

Crashblade watched as the static dissipated from the pile of ash. "The roots have already broken through to the ninth level. We've got hundreds of breaches all over this level of the city already. I've got nearly the whole force trying to keep them at bay, but we're losing the battle."

As he said this, another root grew out from the fracture in the ceiling and pushed its way into the open air. The commander raised his plasma thrower and fired the weapon at the appendage. Liquid fire shot from the barrel, engulfing the root and melting it to nothing in an instant.

"Like I was saying, at this rate we have two, maybe two and a half days at the most before they'll reach the ground floor," said the commander. "Tonight I'm going to declare an emergency and bring in the Civilian Guard."

Enob agreed. "I've already contacted Greylok. Our Elf Nation should have reinforcements here first thing in the morning."

The radio on the commander's belt buzzed, and

he answered it. "This is Crashblade. Slow down…what's the situation? Okay, I got it…yes, I understand completely…. We'll be right over."

The commander turned to Enob. "A big root just broke through at Keelington Towers. They need our help."

The two of them jumped into an IEA-issued hover-car and took off in a flurry of ash and flashing blue lights. Crashblade gunned the accelerator, and they sped off across the parking deck to the edge of the lot and into free air. When the ground fell away beneath them, Crashblade kicked the car's powerful thrusters into full gear and expertly merged the car into the chaos of aerial transport all around them. He weaved in and out of traffic, jumping between the designated lanes, passing cars from above and below as well as to the left and right.

In complete contrast with his usual steady demeanor, Enob was white-knuckled in the passenger seat, pressing down hard on an imaginary brake.

"WATCH out for the BUS—I mean the TAXI…! No, No the air-cycle…! OHHH, we're going to

DIIIEEE!!!"

Completely relaxed and seemingly oblivious to both the traffic and Enob's ravings, Crashblade dialed in the coordinates for Keelington Towers and switched the radio to a classical station. Enjoying the music of one of the great local composers, he finally glanced over at Enob.

"Sorry, I was flipping through the stations. What were you saying?"

Fox looked over his shoulder at his companions as he pushed on the gate set in the fence. It opened with a squeak, and they stepped onto the path to the house. Just as the gate swung shut behind them, a figure appeared in the open doorway.

The Tooth Faerie was beautiful beyond words. She had perfect white-porcelain skin with rosy red cheeks. Her hair flowed down her back, exquisite burnished locks that looked as if they could have been spun from real gold. She was wearing an elegant long white dress that hugged her figure perfectly and accentuated her dainty features. When she smiled it seemed the whole world got a little brighter around them.

With a long, gloved hand she gestured for them to come in. As they stepped onto the porch, a fat, orange-striped cat whooshed past the companions and brushed up against the Tooth Faerie's leg, giving Murdox a long, lazy smile.

"Welcome to my humble home. Please, why don't you come in," said the Tooth Faerie in a smooth, pleasant voice.

Kestrel smiled and stepped over the threshold, followed by the others.

The inside of the house was as quaint as the outside. The room they were standing in was large and airy, with bright yellow walls, vaulted ceilings, and ornately carved wooden fixtures. The furniture looked comfortable and homey, well padded and pleasing to the eye. A few chairs lined the walls, and a long couch embroidered in a flowery pattern sat near the middle of the room. Everything was brought together with colorful artwork and finely woven throw rugs that were placed with care around the charming space.

Kase moved to the center of the room and nudged Murdox in the side, speaking just under his breath. "What's the big deal? This looks nice."

Ever so slightly Murdox curled back his lip and exposed a long canine tooth that he was sure the cat would see. "Exactly. Everything here is way too nice…much, much too nice."

For a moment the Tooth Faerie surveyed them from the doorway and sneered at Murdox, slamming the door behind them. "Way too nice, indeed!" screamed the beautiful faerie.

The wolf-dog looked at the young agent and groaned. *"Here we go…."*

The Tooth Faerie started to grin, but when the grin should have stopped, her lips just kept expanding until a fissure opened from one side of her face to the other, exposing row after row of pointy white teeth. Her body began to vibrate violently, tearing her dress to shreds and shaking the skin loose from her small frame. Her body twisted and stretched into inhuman proportions, convulsing as her arms and legs grew far longer than it seemed should have been possible. Her golden locks flew out in clumps, leaving behind a head of matted, greasy black hair.

Her beautiful eyes expanded diagonally and burned from within with yellow faerie fire. She stood on wobbly legs, now looking far more like a ghoul than a beautiful faerie.

Laughing at their shocked faces, the fiend waved her bony hand around the room.

"Yesh, indeed. Velcome to my beautiful home!"

All around the little company, the false façade of the cottage fell away. The yellow walls melted, exposing moldy stone walls infested with crawling insects. The furniture fell to the floor in heaps of dust and splintered wood, leaving behind structures that looked more like bone than anything else. The artwork and beautiful rugs dissolved and unraveled, becoming nothing more than blackened pulp and piles of filthy yarn.

The orange-striped cat that they had seen when they arrived leapt onto a moldy stone table and hissed at Murdox. Where its fur had been a minute before was now nothing more than ragged clumps of dirty brown hair attached to skin that was pulled far too tight over its skeletal frame.

Kase looked around at what had just become a nightmare. "I'm thinking that I don't want to ask about Santa Claus, do I?"

Murdox took his eye off the skeletal cat for just a moment and looked up at the boy. "Nope...no, you most certainly don't."

Crashblade and Enob arrived at Keelington Towers and landed the hover-car in a designated location near the entrance to the building. IEA officials were forced to move away a crowd of onlookers that had gathered around the scene and make a path for the commander and the wizard to pass.

The building was wrapped in a mass of twisting, brown roots that wove around the structure, adhering to walls and breaking through windows as it got a firm hold on the building. Surrounding the base of the building, a team of agents burned through the roots with their plasma throwers and chemical weapons in an attempt to keep them from growing any further. By the time Enob and the commander reached the other agents, it was apparent that they were already losing the battle.

Crashblade grabbed the shoulder of a huge black-bear humanoid that was brandishing a harness-mounted Gatling gun. "What's the status, soldier?"

The bear-man grabbed a clip of ammunition from a bandoleer of artillery crisscrossing his chest and slammed it into the weapon's magazine. "We've got ourselves a feeder line here, sir," he replied. "We've been working the spot for hours, but we're losing ground. The troops are exhausted, and we're running out of ammo." The soldier hesitated. "Sir, if I may ask, sir? Why haven't we sent troops into the Park? We could cut this off at the nub and end it."

Crashblade looked out over the devastation all around him. "We thought of that, but ever since the blackout, the portal between the Park and Cloudview has been failing. The magic that holds the quantum field together must have been compromised when the Tree stole the power from the city. It fell completely, shortly after Enob passed through it. To try now would be suicide."

Suddenly a root broke free just over the bear-man's head, and the agent spun around, firing his gun at it point blank. The five barrels of the weapon exploded in a rush of destruction, shredding away any remnants of life, as well as a huge chunk of the building.

The soldier turned back to the commander with the barrels of the gun still smoldering in his massive paws. "Sorry about that, sir. I guess I'm getting a little shell-shocked, as well."

Cringing, the commander patted him on the armored shoulder. "No problem, son. Just keep up the good work."

All around them new roots liberated themselves from the structure and pushed ever closer to the ground. Enob grabbed hold of one with his bare hand and burned it into ash with his magical touch.

"We're just about to loose this level of the city," he said. "At this rate we're going to lose the war if our friends don't hurry up."

Crashblade stared at the smoking root in Enob's

hand and shook his head in despair.

The Tooth Faerie grabbed Murdox by the jaw and pulled back his upper lip, exposing most of his canine teeth. "Nice…. It's not that often I find a healthy set of wolf fangs. They'll make a nice addition to my little collection."

The old hag moved next to Kase and rubbed her gnarled hand over the boy's cheek, pulling back his lip. "Well, well, well…if it isn't Justin Kasey Hobskin. I haven't seen these choppers since you lost your two front teeth." She cackled as if that was some kind of hilarious joke. "The permanent teeth have come in well, but I'd get that bicuspid on the left checked. Looks like you might have a cavity starting."

Kase backed off slightly and grinned. "Yeah, I guess just a bit too much candy…and probably not enough flossing."

The Tooth Faerie drew back from the company and stroked the skeletal spine of her cat, which elicited a raspy purr from the misshapen creature. "To what do I owe this pleasure? Maybe you want to see my collection?"

Kestrel took a brave step forward. "We need your help to get to the Faerie Queen's castle. She's got one of the two staves of power and is trying to re-grow the Tree."

The Tooth Faerie grinned, giving them all a good view of her razor-edged teeth. "Yes, yes I can feel the power of the Tree already. Soon it will be too strong to stop...but what does this have to do with me?"

Murdox took over. "If the Queen succeeds, and the Tree is reborn, who can say what will happen to the way magic works in this world. As a former wizard, I know a little bit about the stuff, and I'd bet you one of my teeth that your illusions won't be the same...and I'm pretty sure dimensional travel will be all messed up." He gave her a moment to think about the ramifications, then continued. "How are you going to keep your little tooth business going if you can't get around the dimensions, and especially if you look as unpleasant as you do now? I've got to tell you...you're uglier than even a mother could love."

The Tooth Faerie twisted her fingers around a

necklace of strung teeth, and finally nodded, clapping her hands together. As soon as she had done this, the cottage began to knit back together all around them. The walls renewed themselves and were soon back to a nice shade of yellow. The dust and splinters of the furniture began to re-form and looked comfortable and functional again. The paintings and floor coverings melded back together and were once more stylish. Every little detail was the same as before—even the cat was fat and happy again. The Tooth Faerie smiled with her pearly whites…but somehow this time the world didn't seem quite as bright as before.

The beautiful faerie glided to the back of the cottage and waved her hand in front of the farthest wall. An invisible door appeared, and the Tooth Faerie stepped through. The little company followed her into an enormous space that extended in either direction for as far as the eye could see. In this room thousands upon thousands of huge barrels were stored, each nearly overflowing with teeth of every shape and variety.

The area also housed a giant coin press, operated by little winged men. Currently the machine

Sidhe

was pounding away, stamping out silver dollars that had a picture of a unicorn on one side and the face of some monarch on the other. One of the little winged pixies beamed and flicked a coin over to Kase, which he caught in his hand.

"Looks like you've got your own mint here," said the young agent as he contemplated reporting this information to the Tax Division of the IEA.

The Tooth Faerie grinned. "Yes, I can produce a coin for hundreds of known dimensions." As if she read the boy's thoughts, she continued, "Don't worry. Its all on the up and up. Most of the money goes back into the economy. The toy retailers are particularly happy. I just like to do my part and keep the economic engine running smoothly."

As she led the company down a passage between the barrels of teeth, she turned back to face them.

"So, how can I help you?"

"I understand that you're the gatekeeper of one end of a tunnel that leads from here to the Queen's castle," said Kestrel. "We've tried to pass through the forest to reach the Tree, but she has it well guarded and magically protected to keep trespassers out."

The faerie nodded. "Yes, I can feel her power,. She's growing very strong. I'm even having trouble resisting her spell."

Along the back wall of the vast room was a line of small offices, each occupied by one of the little winged pixies that they had seen running the coin press. The Tooth Faerie paused at one of the doors and pushed it open. In the office was a beautiful wooden desk with a computing machine on it. There was also a comfortable sofa and some chairs.

She eyed the group and smiled. "Have a seat, and we'll discuss our terms."

The wolf-dog growled. "Why do I have bad feeling about this?"

The Tooth Faerie took a seat behind her desk and looked all of them over once more. "I'll let you pass and even give you a key to unlock the door on the other side, but I'll require a small payment for this service." She paused. "I'd like a few of those pointy canines of yours, Murdox."

Sidhe

The wolf-dog growled. "If you think I'm going to give any up that easy...you're going to have to pry my teeth out of your leg with your own hands!"

Fox and Kestrel grabbed the hilts of their weapons, but Kase calmed them all down.

"Hold on! I think I might have something here that she might want. Just give me a second to look in my bag."

The boy slipped his pack off his back, unzipped the flap, and dug around through its contents for a while, finally emerging with what he wanted.

"How about this?" asked the boy.

The Tooth Faerie's eyes glowed green with an inner fire that almost blinded them. She could hardly contain her excitement. "Wherever did you get that? Of all the millions of teeth I have, I don't have one of those. I've been trying for centuries but haven't even gotten close. What you have in your hand is one of the most precious of all the teeth in the known dimensions. She opened a drawer in her desk "Here! Here's the key. Just give me the tooth!"

Kase held the tooth up to her but snatched it

away again before she could grab it. "We need a map. I doubt any of us trust you to lead us through the tunnels, so we're going to need a good map."

The Tooth Faerie leapt up from her desk and unlocked a cabinet on the wall, retrieving a dusty old book. Blowing the dust off the cover, she flipped it open and found the page she was looking for. Taking the book to a nearby copying machine, she opened the lid and smiled at Kase. "Just let it warm up for a second," she said.

With a whirr, the machine lit up, and she placed the book on the glass.

"Look. There we go…the latest map of the tunnels. It should just do the trick."

Kase took the map and let Kestrel and Fox look it over.

"Looks good," said Kestrel, with Fox nodding his approval, as well.

Kase opened his fist and handed the faerie the tooth. In turn she handed him the golden key and waved her hand in front of the bookcase. The case slid away, revealing a hidden door, which she opened with another key that was hanging from a hook on the wall.

With gloved hands the Tooth Faerie gently took the tooth and placed it delicately on a velvet cloth on her desk. Completely ignoring the little group, she pulled a magnifying jeweler's loupe from her drawer and began a through examination of the piece.

Fox shrugged and gestured to Kestrel through the open door, and without a word they stepped into the tunnel. Just as they all crossed over the threshold, the door slammed shut with an audible thud.

Kase pulled some flashlights from his pack and handed them out.

Murdox looked up at the boy with what Kase thought was a tear in his eye. "That was beautiful, man. I'm so proud…."

Fox and Kestrel patted the young agent on the shoulder.

"Good job!" said Fox. "That kept us out of a fight that we didn't need."

"What kind of tooth was it that you gave her, anyway?" asked the young Sentinel.

Kase grinned. "One from a blood dragon. I've

got a couple more in my bag. Who would have thought they were so valuable. One man's junk is another man's treasure, I guess."

-Chapter Fourteen-
A World Beneath

Wave after blue wave of electric energy rippled across the roots, shriveling them to a crisp. Ash and soot fell from the sky, covering everything in a blanket of black and gray.

Another root grew outward from a crack not two feet from where the wizard had just destroyed the last one. Enob raised his hands once more to try again, but they were swollen and charred from the countless times he had released his magic.

The wizard fell to his knees, exhausted, and called out to the commander, "After so many hours, I'm afraid I don't have much left in me."

Crashblade fired his plasma gun at the tangle of roots, surrounding them with liquid flame until the barrel of his weapon glowed red from the heat. He looked out over the city, but all he could see was ash.

Just as he thought they might have stemmed the tide of the infestation, a new batch of roots emerged from the charred walls and ceilings.

They were standing at the base of one of the main support buildings for this city level and were only seconds from losing the building to the infestation from the Tree. It wasn't for lack of trying, though. Every able-bodied soul from each level was pitching in to stop the downward growth, but it couldn't be stopped, only slowed.

It was a frustrating battle. When one of the roots had been cleared away, another sprang up in its place. Magic and technology had each been expended unchecked, incinerating the roots but at the same time blasting holes in the city's structures.

Crashblade shut down his weapon to let it cool and sat next to Enob. He looked around at the damage they had done and lost a little more hope. "Even if we save the city from the Tree, the damage we've caused here will take years to fix."

Enob sighed. "What you say is true, but from what I've determined, the alternative would be much worse."

They both looked up at the surrounding buildings, all entangled in roots, and moaned. They were on the third level of the vast multi-city metropolis of Cloudview, and at any moment they could lose this city, as well, to the giant Tree. From the thirteenth level down, each city had been claimed by the roots. The buildings and structures had all been overrun with the creeping offshoots, and the citizens of the cities were forced to evacuate, creating a tense, near-panic atmosphere throughout Cloudview as a whole.

Crashblade fired his weapon at a nearby root and then lowered it and sighed as he watched the ashes descend. "This level's lost, too. We only have the first and second levels left before the roots hit the ground, and then it'll be over, and we'll lose the war to the Tree."

Enob looked down at his smoking hands. "If Kestrel's team doesn't get to the Tree in the next couple of days, its magic will be too strong to resist. It will claim all of Cloudview and will change the world as we know it."

Crashblade hoisted his gun again. "We can only try to slow down the progress and hope they can get to it in time."

He checked the plasma clip on his weapon and tapped it with his finger. "I'm just about out of ammunition, and I'm also physically worn out to the point that I can hardly stand, either. There really isn't anything else we can do here anyway. Let's take a short break and then get down to the second level."

Fox recalled some of his lessons regarding the different races. "Assuming this really is a prison for fae folk, and they have been living down here for ages, then we're going to have some real trouble on our hands. I don't know if we'll be able to avoid them altogether, but we need to do our best and get through this without losing any more time."

Kestrel agreed. "The faeries have swift minds and keen ears, and down here they will have adapted as best they can to survive. They've probably become pretty ruthless hunters and may live in a fairly lawless society. From now on we'll really need to be on our guard."

They had been walking for nearly the whole day and were now deep under the mountain. The dim glow of their flashlights illuminated the cavern walls. This was the world beneath the Park. Here there was no sky or fresh air, only the hard, cold rock all around them. In this dark realm, the tunnels extended under the mountains for hundreds of miles, through winding passages that connected many large and small caverns. In this world of heartless stone, the silence was overwhelming, only to be broken once in a great while by a distant plop of water as it fell into some lost pool and echoed through the maze of tunnels.

Occasionally the beam from Kase's flashlight would break the monotonous darkness and illuminate some kind of phosphorescent fungus that glowed an eerie green under the minimal light. They found that they could actually see by that glow, and when they came across long stretches of fungus, they would extinguish their portable lights to conserve the batteries.

Finally Murdox broke the silence and sat back on his haunches, scratching the back of his ear with a paw. "Oh, I'm so glad I've got such a cool job that takes me to these exotic places."

Kase patted him on the top of his head. "Well, what can I say…maybe the next one will be to the beach."

Kestrel turned on her flashlight and pointed it down onto the map. The two elves studied the lines and figures for a few moments and both indicated agreement.

"According to this map, we've made good time. Without it I fear we might have been stuck down here for much longer. At this pace we should be able to clear the tunnel by late tomorrow," said Kestrel.

Kase yawned and Murdox's stomach growled. "Could we take a rest for a little while and maybe grab a bite of food?" asked Kase. "The last few days have been quite hard on this wolf-dog and me, and I'm sure Murdox is famished."

Fox nodded approval. "Of course. I'm a bit hungry and tired, as well. The tunnel should widen out just ahead, and we can eat and rest for a few hours."

After a light meal, they unrolled their sleeping bags and found a small niche in the rock wall to rest. A few hours later, Fox shot up from his bag when his keen elf ears alerted him to danger.

Click, click, click.

"What was that?" asked Murdox

Kestrel and Fox already had their weapons drawn.

"Kase, leave your flashlight off for the moment," said Fox. "Kestrel and I will shift our eyesight to infrared so we can pick up any heat signatures. It will help us get a better feel for what we're up against."

Click, click, click.

"That was from behind us," said Murdox.

Click, click, click.

"And that was from in front of us," said Kase.

Fox felt a slight deviation in the pressure around him, and he knew something was close.

"Kestrel, I can't see anything. Can you?"

"No I can't, either, but I can feel them all around," replied the elf scout.

The air rushed in front of Fox, and he barely blocked a hand that was about to tear into his face with filthy nails. "They're camouflaged in the infrared range! Shift back to the normal spectrum! Kase, turn on your flashlight!"

The young agent did as he was told and shined the beam just in front of Fox and Kestrel. The two elves were back to back and surrounded by hideous pale-white creatures.

Click, click…!

An attack came at Kestrel, and it caught her on the shoulder, but she shifted her stance just enough to prevent it from landing solidly.

The figures were more or less hairless humanoids with nearly translucent white skin. There were no eyes in their smooth, featureless faces—only two small slits for their olfactory senses. Their small mouths were full of needle-like teeth, and they had long, pointed ears that stuck out from their heads.

One of them had crawled across the ceiling above Fox's head and was prepared to drop onto the young Sentinel when Kase hit it with the light. Just as it dropped to the floor, Fox spotted it in his peripheral vision and easily knocked it across the tunnel.

More followed behind the first, crawling on the dirt in front of them as well as around them on the walls and ceiling. Soon they were surrounded by the faceless creatures. The air filled with the strange clicking sounds, and they attacked as one with long, filthy fingers that grasped for the two elves, trying frantically to bring them to the ground.

Suddenly the light in the tunnel went out, and they heard Murdox growl and Kase yell for help. Kestrel and Fox tried to get to them, but there were too many creatures surrounding them to make a clear path.

Fox yelled out as a sea of the creatures came down upon him. "Kase, Murdox, touch the walls whenever you can…we'll be able to follow the heat signatures you leave behind."

With the light source gone and their infrared vision useless against this foe, the two elves had to fall back on their years of training and fight with their other senses. Fox closed his eyes and quieted his mind, allowing his training to take over. Almost instantly he reached a trance-like state in which his mind was calm, yet fully aware of the minutest details around him.

The Sentinel's sword became an extension of his body. Each swing of the blade blended and fused with the next in a deadly dance. Fox responded to every attack with a duck or twist that brought him out of harm's way, at the same time swinging his blade and smiting everything within its reach. The path of the blade defined a sphere around the young Sentinel, generating a dynamic convergence that drew the attacks inward and into the arc of his weapon.

One by one Fox led the creatures to him as he whirled and twirled, spinning in myriad directions while he moved back and forth within the circular pattern. Rank upon rank of the beasts fell at his feet, piling one on top of the other until the final two creatures made their charge.

The fiends could hear the blood flowing in the elves' veins as it pumped efficiently through their bodies. It had been days since the creatures had last eaten, and they were weakened from a lack of food. Using echolocation and smell, they had tracked the party to this tunnel, and without concern for their own safety, they had attacked the strangers. Within these tunnels they were both hunters and scavengers. They would feed on whatever they could find, but in the worst of times they would resort to cannibalism.

The last two creatures dove at Fox, racing toward the sound of his beating heart. The young Sentinel surged forward, breaking out of his sphere just as both of the creatures grabbed for him. He dove to the ground and rolled over his shoulder, springing up behind them just as they passed by. By the time they realized what had happened, it was already too late for them.

-Chapter Fifteen-
Off to the Races

Fox turned to help Kestrel, but there was no need. She had taken down scores of the foul beasts that now lay injured all around her. The rest had fled the scene…or had fallen to an even worse fate. Fox shuddered at the sight.

"Do you have any idea in which direction they took Kase and Murdox?"

Before she answered, she first allowed her eyes to shift out of the normal visible spectrum into the infrared. "Look down the tunnel. I think that's a paw print."

They raced down the tunnel and found a series of paw prints and what almost looked like an arrow scratched in the dirt.

"Good! I'm glad they heard us," said Kestrel. "Let's hope they kept it up. This way they'll be easy to track."

They followed the cooling prints down the tunnels. Some were on the walls, others on low-hanging ceilings, but each one was visible enough to follow. For nearly an hour the elves followed the glowing trail. They were moving fast but still couldn't catch up with the creatures. This was their home, and they knew how to get around in it.

They stopped when the tunnel branched ahead of them, and Fox held up his hand, hesitating at the intersection. The trail lead down the passage to the left, but they could hear the strange clicking sounds, as well as voices intermixed with sounds of a struggle.

Kase thrashed in the clutches of the beast. Both he and Murdox had been dragged from the fight, kicking and screaming. They had yelled for help, but Kestrel and Fox were too heavily engaged in battle to come to their aid. Numerous times the boy tried to reach his blaster in the holster on his belt, but one of the fiends had the young agent flung over his back in such a way that he couldn't quite get to it.

It was pitch black, and he quickly became disorientated, with no idea which way was up or down. The creature could crawl over the walls or ceilings as easily as it could on the ground, and this activity began to take its toll on the boy's stomach. For what felt like an eternity, he had been carried this way from one tunnel to the next, doing his best to mark the walls and ceilings with his hands. When they stopped to negotiate an obstacle, he would let his stomach catch up while he used the extra few seconds to trace the shape of an arrow marking their direction.

Even without light he could sense that he was surrounded by these foul creatures. Occasionally they would bump into him and he could feel their skin. It was smooth, not slimy or snakelike—more closely resembling that of a salamander—and they smelled of the earth, slightly moldy, the way it does after a rainstorm.

Kase heard Murdox behind him, struggling with his captors, as well.

"Murdox, are you okay?"

The wolf-dog growled and said, "For the

moment, but we need to get out of here before they decide to have an evening meal. Can you get to your gun?"

Kase tried again to reach his weapon. "No, I've been trying, but I can't reach it. His arm's in the way, and I can't make it budge…."

The monster grabbed the young agent by the hood of his sweatshirt and pulled the boy around to face him—close enough that he could smell its fetid breath. The beast shook Kase violently while clicking in his face, and Kase shut his mouth.

The two elves heard Murdox howl in the distance, and they knew they were getting close. They took off at a dead run in the direction of the wolf-dog, but as they closed in on the sounds, they realized that the tunnel was growing brighter, and they allowed their eyes to shift back to the visible spectrum. They emerged in a large cavern lit by hundreds of lanterns that glowed the same eerie shade of green that the fungus did. The strange light cast long shadows as it illuminated huge stalactites and stalagmites that clung to the ceiling and rose up from the floor in menacing shapes. They couldn't spy a clear path through the cavern, as it was littered with fallen rocks and boulders that stood as tall as grown men, and they knew this wasn't going to be easy.

Fox had just ducked behind a fallen stalactite when his sixth sense alerted him to danger. An instant later a long, thin dart imbedded itself in the rock only inches from his head.

Kestrel sensed the danger as well and was already on the move, leaping between two massive boulders as a volley of projectiles hit just behind her. She peered up from between the rocks to survey the scene.

The good news was that the creatures that had captured Kase and Murdox now seemed to be having their own troubles. The bad news was that gray-skinned faeries now surrounded Kase and Murdox's kidnappers, shooting at them with darts and crossbow bolts. By sheer numbers many of the faceless white creatures had escaped the trap and had gone on the offensive, struggling in hand-to-hand combat with the faeries, dragging them to the ground.

For the most part, faeries resembled elves in physical appearance and characteristics, having descended from the same original Sídhe stock. Both were fleet-footed, with keen senses and physical strength that exceeded their size relative to humans. The most obvious difference between the two distinct variations was the color of their skin. While elves tended to have skin and hair color similar to humans, most faerie folk that lived above ground ranged in skin color from a pale green to a gray-brown, and their hair had a distinctly leafy texture, with colors that varied from shades of green or yellow to a deep red-brown, depending on the season of the year.

The variant of faerie that lived below the ground was somewhat different. Their skin ranged from a dark gray to a deep black, with long, mud-colored hair that changed tones and highlights relative to the surrounding stone walls. To the unfamiliar eye, they appeared more like shadows, and they avoided the light whenever possible. As Kestrel had surmised, they had grown accustomed to the darkness and adapted to live in it, and their personalities and ideals had adapted, as well. They'd become wicked and malicious. No longer did they seek the light, as did their brethren above ground. Now they preferred the darkness.

The gray-skinned faerie warriors wore black armor that flexed and shifted silently with every move they made. Each carried with him a blowgun or a crossbow and a short staff with curved blades on both ends. Ten of them fought in the cavern against no less than thirty of the faceless horrors. Their trap had given them the upper hand, but they were outnumbered, and the tide was about to turn.

Out of nowhere, twenty of the dark-skinned fae folk entered the battle, attacking both the creatures and the gray faeries. They were all apparently in the midst of some civil war or territorial dispute, but just what it was really didn't matter to the elves. Right now they had only one objective, and that was to retrieve Kase and Murdox and then get back to the surface.

Two faeries riding on the backs of lizards spotted the fallen boy and the wolf-dog between the rocks. Their sure-footed reptilian mounts easily navigated the rocks and boulders, bounding from one to the next as they rushed over to investigate this curious turn of events. Hardly slowing his steed, one faerie grabbed Kase by an arm and slung him on the back of the reptile.

The boy struggled to break free, kicking and pounding with his feet and hands, but the faerie grabbed a yellow-tipped dart from his pouch and jabbed it into the young agent's leg. The last thing Kase remembered before slipping into unconsciousness was Murdox chasing after him and yelling something particularly vulgar at his captor.

The lizard-back faerie that was after Murdox was not nearly so lucky. The dog was ready for the attack and easily avoided one of the darts that was shot at him. When the faerie got close enough, Murdox leapt up on his powerful hind legs and snapped at the rider, taking a big chunk out of his arm and ripping him from his saddle. The rider fell to the ground with a thud and blacked out when his head smashed into a rock.

Suddenly Murdox felt a sharp sting in his flank and realized he had been hit with a dart. The wolf-dog turned his head and spotted a third faerie approaching on its lizard but was too weak to resist when it grabbed him by the scruff of his neck and tossed him onto the creature's back.

Fox pointed in the direction Kase and Murdox were taken and shouted, "Over there! Those faeries riding lizard-back just grabbed our friends."

Kestrel had seen it as well and called back, "I'm closer to Murdox. I'll go after him, and you get Kase."

Fox nodded and took off in the direction of the kidnappers. He avoided two of the faceless creatures by sliding between them and leaping over a small chasm to the relative safety of a boulder about ten feet above where Kase was. He was caught off guard by a faerie but realized that it was looking in the opposite direction. The Sentinel didn't need an arrow in his posterior, so he slammed into the backside of the dark-skinned faerie, easily knocking him between the rocks.

The young Sentinel didn't stop again until he was surrounded by three more of the evil faeries, but before they could attack, two of the white fiends surprised them by climbing up between the boulders, grabbing them by the legs, and pulling them down to the ground below. The remaining faerie warriors charged at Fox, but the Sentinel sidestepped the attack and pushed one from behind as he passed by. The agile faerie rolled away from the fall and leapt to his feet, spinning back in the direction of the elf, but the young Sentinel was already gone. The faerie warrior pulled a small crossbow from his back and loaded the weapon, firing a bolt at Fox.

The Sentinel's sixth sense went wild, and he ducked out of the way at the last second as the bolt shot passed his head, grazing his shoulder in the process. Fortunately his armor prevented any damage, and he continued his chase across the cavern, vaulting from one boulder to the next.

He spied Kase on the back of the lizard, but the creature was moving fast, easily gliding over the rocky ground. A second later he tensed and shifted his weight, swerving to the right to avoid another missile as it whizzed past his ear, drawing his gaze away from the fleeing reptile. He spotted it again just as it slipped into one of the many connecting tunnels that disappeared off into the darkness of the passage.

Kestrel was faring only slightly better. She pulled her bow from her shoulder and, in a volley of arrows, downed enough of the faeries and white fiends to clear a path through the maze of rocks and boulders. She took off after Murdox and made it nearly halfway before she was stopped by two faeries that sprang up from between the rocks. One had a long metal shaft that was bladed on both ends, and the other wielded a slender, curved sword. Somehow Kestrel was able to avoid the first strike by the swordsman but took a nasty slash to her thigh from the staffed weapon. She cringed in pain but knew that if it weren't for her elven armor, she could have lost a leg.

She ducked the next blow and whirled in place with her sword in hand, slicing the weapon across the knees of the faerie with the double-bladed staff. It knocked the fighter to the ground, and she kicked him off the rock.

The elf scout parried another strike by the

swordsman and made an opening for him to thrust the weapon at her. The faerie took the bait and lunged forward, allowing Kestrel to pivot around the attack on her heels and slide her arm under his. She rotated hard with her hips and threw the faerie off balance, making him stagger back. Before he got a chance to right himself, she wheeled around and finished him off with a roundhouse kick to the gut. A second later she was back on the move, chasing after the lizard that had Murdox.

Fox had reached the tunnel where Kase had been taken and was stopped in mid stride when one of the wretched white creatures dropped from the ceiling. The young Sentinel dipped his head, turned slightly, and rammed the creature in the chest with his shoulder. A dart that was meant for Fox struck the beast in the neck, dropping him to the ground. Fox turned to confront the faerie with the blowgun, but he was already down, with an arrow stuck in his chest. Fox turned on his heels and raced into the tunnel, waving thanks to Kestrel as he disappeared into the darkness.

One Wizard Place

Just as Kestrel had hit the faerie that was about to shoot Fox, another one fired off a shot at her; but luck was on her side as it struck her in the wrist, where she wore a metal bracer that deflected the dart with a ringing sound. Before the faerie realized what had happened, he found an arrow in his chest, as well. The elf scout vaulted over her fallen enemies and found Murdox's kidnapper busy fighting off three of the white fiends as they tried to pull him from his lizard.

With bow in hand, the elf scout eliminated the three translucent white monsters and took aim at the faerie. She released the arrow, but the swift faerie deflected it with a small shield he wore on his arm. She nocked another arrow and positioned herself to fire once more when the faerie pulled a dagger from his belt and threatened to stab the unconscious wolf-dog with it. He smiled a wicked smile but quickly dropped the dagger to the ground when her arrow found his wrist. In the faerie's moment of confusion, Kestrel jumped up onto the lizard's back, knocked him behind the head with her fist, and threw him from the saddle. She checked on Murdox's condition and found him to be

Sidhe

alive…only tranquilized and out cold. Satisfied that he would be fine, she pulled hard on the lizard's reins and pointed the creature toward the tunnel where Fox had run.

-Chapter Sixteen-

Upside-down

The dark-skinned faerie ducked his lizard into a side tunnel just off the main cavern, where he met up with the others from his patrol. Altogether there were five of them, each riding a lizard and each not looking very pleased when they spotted Kestrel on the back of one of their mounts. They watched in dismay as she came straight for them, running the lizard as fast as it could go.

The faerie with Kase tried to get out of the way when he realized she was trying to ram him, but she was coming too fast, and he couldn't move in time. Seconds before crashing into him, the lizard veered off, missing him by a few scant inches. The faerie tried to figure out what had just happened, but before he could get a cognizant thought through his head, another elf crashed into him.

Sidhe

Fox had a razor-edged dagger in his hand when he slipped out from behind Kestrel on her lizard. He leapt directly into the faerie, sliced through his safety harness, and tossed him from the saddle before he even knew what hit him. The young Sentinel pulled hard on that lizard's reins and turned the beast toward the end of the tunnel. Kestrel followed directly behind, kicking her lizard in the sides with her heels to keep pace with him.

Out of the dimness, the void opened up in front of Fox. He pulled back on the reins as hard as he could and stopped only inches from the edge, knocking dirt into the blackness below. Kestrel pulled up next to the young Sentinel, and they peered over the rim. They were greeted by a cold wind blowing up from the depths of the pit and chilling them to the bone. Behind them came the four remaining fighters, hard on their tails.

An arrow struck the wall next to Kestrel's head, and she needed to make a decision fast. That was when the elf scout spotted the lizard's toes. There were three of them, to be exact, and she knew immediately what to do. She pressed her heels into the lizard and pointed it into the pit. Without hesitation the creature complied and stepped off the edge.

The lizard was a slender, eight-foot-long reptile with slate-gray, smooth-textured skin and a long, flexible tail. It had four long legs, each with a three-toed foot that ended in sticky, round pads. The pads, combined with the reptile's incredible agility, made it an excellent climber that could cope with most surfaces at any angle—even upside down.

Kestrel had been too preoccupied to think about what kind of lizard she was riding until they had hit the edge of the chasm. Fortunately that was when she remembered seeing a much smaller variety of these three-toed creatures climbing up and around the walls and windows of her home. She took a big gamble, and it paid off. Without any instruction from its rider, the lizard climbed down to a long bridge that disappeared far off into the distance.

Fox watched Kestrel slip over the edge, and as quick as he could, tied his safety harness around his waist and followed behind. The two elves allowed their eyes to shift into the infrared spectrum, and they were pleased to see that the room was a maze of suspension bridges that spanned gaps between enormous stalactites. The bridges had been lit with some kind of naturally occurring element that glowed within the infrared spectrum, and they assumed that the faeries must have constructed these to link one side of the cavern with the other.

The elves raced down the bridge, trying to get as much distance between themselves and the faerie fighters as possible; but before they had gone fifty steps, the structure shuddered and bounced up and down. In a quick glance to the rear, they spotted the last two faeries leaping from the edge of the escarpment and landing nimbly on the bridge right behind them. In response they pushed their lizards harder but were quickly losing ground to the much more experienced faerie riders.

Kestrel yelled back to Fox, "Let's split up when we get to the first stalactite. That might give us a better chance." Fox tried to reply but lost his concentration when an arrow whizzed past his ear.

Kestrel hit the rock formation first and directed her lizard upward. The creature grabbed onto the rocky wall and easily climbed up, as she pointed the lizard around to the backside of the stalactite and onto another bridge that veered off to the left of the main line. She hit the bridge running, pushing the creature down the wooden planks and ignoring the swaying motion as best she could. Two of the fae riders split off in her direction, still trying to chase her down. She ran the lizard to the end of the short expanse and struck the supporting stalactite hard, pointing the creature to the other side, in the direction of the next linking bridge. Instead of going up, she turned the creature and pointed it down so that it would go directly under the bridge and out of their line of sight.

Fox reached the stalactite and turned to the right, running up the side of the structure until he stumbled upon another bridge that crossed about twenty feet over the main line. His lizard jumped onto the bridge, and they raced across the stretch until he could feel his pursuers right behind him. Fortunately for him, the bridges weren't made to be run across, and they swayed back and forth and up and down on their suspension ropes. This was a very disconcerting feeling but also had a significant advantage: the faeries couldn't get off a clean shot with their arrows or darts. By the time they got close enough to hit him point blank, Fox had made it to the next stalactite and raced down its face until he could see the main-line bridge again. Without waiting for the lizard to climb any farther, he jumped it away from the rocky wall and let it freefall the rest of the way to the bridge.

Kestrel's pursuers climbed down the rock wall and hit the top of the bridge, running its entire length in pursuit of her. The elf scout knew it would be only a few seconds before they realized she had given them the slip, so she turned her mount in the opposite direction. She pointed the three-toed lizard toward the opposite side of the stalactite and climbed back up until she could reach the next bridge and go back in the direction of the main line. When she got within thirty feet of the ceiling, her peripheral vision caught movement from above. She groaned when she discovered that four more of the fae warriors had joined the chase.

Kestrel tried to turn and hoped they hadn't seen her but knew she wouldn't have any such luck. They were completely upside down, trotting across the ceiling as casually as they would on the ground. One of them spotted her right away and pointed her out to the others. The warrior who was apparently their leader directed two of the others to the opposite side of the cavern, and they split off from the group.

Fox had been seen as well. The young Sentinel ran down the bridge, looking behind him to determine where his pursuers had gone. For some unknown reason, they had fallen back and were slowing down. Before he had a chance to contemplate this, two more fae warriors dropped from the ceiling and landed on the bridge about fifty feet in front of him.

Fox was trapped between the two groups and didn't have anywhere else to turn. He looked down and spotted a bridge far below…and had a very scary idea. As hard as he could, he yanked the harness to the left, trying to get the creature to jump; but what happened next, he didn't expect at all. Instead of leaping into the air and probably to an early demise, the lizard grabbed hold of one of the suspension ropes with it tail and flipped over the edge of the bridge so that it was situated upside down on the bottom side of the structure. Slightly relieved, Fox pressed his heals hard into the lizard's flanks, and it raced down the bridge right under the two faerie fighters in front of him.

Kase shook his head to try to clear the fog from his mind. He was trying to wake up from a really bad dream when he realized that he was actually living in a nightmare. For one thing, he was completely disoriented and nauseous, and his head was throbbing like there was no tomorrow. He opened his watery eyes to see if that would help but found that this accomplished nothing but to make him even dizzier than he had already been. The one good thing about all this was he was pretty sure he heard Fox's voice and that he was the one driving this crazy ride.

"Fox…is that you up there?"

The Sentinel turned his head ever so slightly and called back, "Yup."

"Well, that's one good thing," said the boy. He felt the top of his head and realized that his hair was floating at a strange angle. "Are we upside down?"

"Yup."

Kase made a quick check that he was firmly secured in. "I was better off unconscious, wasn't I?"

The elf pulled the reins hard to the right, taking the lizard into a high g-force maneuver. "Yup."

Kase's stomach lurched and he called back, "Just checking. I'll be quite now."

From what he could tell, it was pretty much a bad day.

Kestrel scrambled her lizard vertically up the stalactite to the ceiling and went upside down, pointing it in the direction of the main line, away from her two new threats. She positioned herself so that the rock formation was between her and them, hopefully buying some time and gaining cover from any arrows or darts that might come her way.

Of course the two dark-skinned faeries that had been chasing her from the beginning had spotted her again and resumed their chase. Before she had made any real progress, the two on the ceiling made it around the rock formation and met up with the first two riders. Now all four of them were pretty much right behind her and closing in fast. Their lead rider pointed to his left and then to his right, and the outer two broke away from the group, apparently splitting up in an attempt to flank her on either side.

The elf scout raced her lizard in a serpentine maneuver, changing her direction every so often to avoid being hit by any flying projectiles, but she wasn't having too much success with this technique.

Thwack, thump, thwack, thump!

From all around her arrows fired and hit the ceiling, missing her by only inches. She was lucky that all of them missed her head, but a few found their marks and lodged into her back and shoulder armor, piercing her skin and drawing blood, but not causing any serious damage. She realized that with one good shot, she could be done for.

Murdox woke up in about the same condition as

Kase. His head pounded, and he was just about to toss his cookies. Unfortunately, his canine vision allowed him to see in the semi-darkness, which wasn't always such a good thing. When he realized he was upside down and riding on the back of a lizard, he let out a howl that scared everyone within shouting distance half to death. Then when an arrow pierced the saddle just below where he was sitting, he passed right back out again.

Fox slipped by directly below two riders and hightailed it under the bridge, gaining a good bit of distance on those warriors while they negotiated turning themselves around. This also created a nice little traffic jam, which kept the other two riders from gaining any distance, as well. As he left his pursuers behind, the young Sentinel spotted Kestrel far above as she tried to evade the four lizards chasing after her, but from his location there was little he could do but watch.

Kestrel made it to the main line only seconds before they would have caught up with her. She leaped off the ceiling and, like a cat, rolled over in the air and landed on the bridge feet-first. She hit just ahead of Fox, nearly knocking him off of the bottom of the bridge, but an arrow struck one of the suspension lines next to her, and she realized that there was no time to apologize.

The warriors on the ceiling started to follow but hesitated when they realized that they had gained an advantage. They knew that the elves would be slowed by the bridge, and the far-more-experienced riders figured that they could get ahead of them and block off the exit.

The end of the bridge came into view, and Kestrel thought that the possibility of getting out of this alive might just be a reality. Then the four fighters dropped down from the ceiling and ruined everything. All four of them hit hard, landing about a hundred feet in front of Kestrel. Two of them split off—one going to the right, the other to the left—and both flipped their lizards around the bridge just like Fox had earlier, blocking the Sentinel's escape as well. The elves looked behind them, and the remaining four pursuers did the same thing. Two lizards on top and two on the bottom—there was nowhere to go.

Fox looked down, but he was greeted only by the blackness of the pit. There was probably a bridge somewhere down there, but he had no idea where. He pulled on the reins, and the lizard climbed up to the top of the bridge.

He yelled to Kestrel in the Elvish tongue, hoping their adversaries might not understand.

"Leap frog, and help me out when you can."

Kestrel smiled and kicked her lizard in the sides as hard as she dared. The creature reared up and yowled before racing forward like wild bull. She slapped the reins and kept jabbing her heels into the creature's sides, not giving it a chance to think or slow down. They slammed right into the lizard in front of her without giving the rider any time to react. Full bore, her three-toed reptile plowed right on top of the other lizard, knocking it senseless and knocking out its fae rider completely. At the same time she used the dazed lizard as a jumping platform and leapt into the air over the second beast, coming down ruthlessly on its tail. This gave her the opportunity she needed, and she ran

Sidhe

toward the exit.

Unfortunately this left Fox in a really bad situation. The two Sídhe riders on the bottom of the bridge reacted to the situation and tried climbing up and around the structure to get at the remaining elf on top.

Fox untied his safety harness, and yelled back to Kase, "Stay here! I'll be right back."

Still blinded by the utter darkness, Kase couldn't see a thing that was going on. He knew only that Fox had leapt away from his saddle.

Fox dove feet-first into the pursuing lizard and rotated forward, slamming his elbow into the faerie rider and knocking him backwards over his saddle. With plenty of momentum to spare, the elf dove over the back of the creature and caught hold of its tail, swinging around so that he could grab the planking on the underside of the bridge. Hand over hand he pulled himself to the other side of the bridge and swung back topside. The second faerie was still looking to see what had happened to the elf when he was struck in the back with enough force to knock the wind from his lungs. The Sentinel pulled his sword from its sheath and raced to the remaining lizard as the faerie warrior aimed his blowgun at him pointblank.

Kestrel removed a long, white arrow from her quiver and nocked it into the bow. She was situated at the exit to the cavern, more than a hundred yards from Fox, when she drew back the bow and released the arrow. Effortlessly it sailed through the air in a gentle arc as it raced toward its target.

As fast as he could, Fox twisted to the side, trying to avoid the fae attacker's dart, but he knew he was just too close to avoid getting hit. A full second passed, and the young Sentinel thought he was done for, but nothing happened until the faerie fell forward with a gleaming white arrow stuck in his back.

Fox thanked his lucky stars and ran back to Kase, leaping into the saddle and urging their lizard forward before the four remaining faeries could respond. The elf needn't have worried, though; after four more perfectly placed arrows from Kestrel none of their pursuers was in any position to keep up the chase.

-Chapter Seventeen-
The Bottom Line

Crashblade pointed his plasma gun downward and pulled hard on the trigger, turning the ground near him into a pool of molten rock. The Tree had reached the first level of the city of Cloudview and was now only inches from contact with the planet's soil.

For thirteen levels below the Park, the Tree had broken through the base of each city, encompassing the ceiling below it in a canopy of leaves and branches that had completely overtaken each level. The citizens had been evacuated, forced to leave Cloudview to escape the growing threat. Every city from the thirteenth level down had been abandoned; the homes and businesses had become nothing more than a tangle of roots and vines that were growing at an extraordinary rate and destroying everything around them in the process. All that remained were the exhausted agents of the Incantation Enforcement Agency, trying in one last stand to stem the tide and buy a little more time.

For days countless volunteers from every city aided the IEA in their continuing struggle to stop the Tree's roots from reaching the ground level. Once the Tree hit firm soil it would be able to absorb the energy from the planet's core to fuel its growth and would become unstoppable. Now the fight was nearly over. By order of the High Mayor, the lower levels of Cloudview had been evacuated. If the worst came to pass, the rest of the vast metropolis would be, as well.

Commander Crashblade tripped over a piece of broken concrete and fell to his knees, cursing. Enob grabbed him by the shoulders to help him to his feet, but the wizard's hands burned into the commander's jacket, searing his skin.

Crashblade winced in pain and got up. All around him stood the last of his weary agents. They were like ants surrounded by the colossal buildings of the lower level. Each building was designed to be a pillar of support for the weight of the entire structure of

Cloudview, thousands of feet above them, but the buildings had been completely entwined in roots, squeezing them like a boa constrictor would its prey.

The agents fired at the roots with the last of their ammunition. Every conceivable weapon, magical device, and spell had been used to stop the roots—enough energy to have leveled a mountain—but all they had been able to do was slow their progress. Every time a weapon ceased firing, another tendril would slip through and get ever closer to the ground.

A young, soot-stained lieutenant staggered up to the commander. "Sir, we've been at this for days and would go on for more if we could," he said, "but the ammunition is running seriously low. Every time we stop to reload, the roots gain another foothold."

Crashblade nodded to the man and asked, "How much ammo is left?"

The exhausted lieutenant hesitated for a moment, trying to do the math in his head, then replied, "The armory is empty. Maybe six or seven hours, at this rate."

Crashblade turned his weapon to a root a few

feet from his head and obliterated it, leaving only ash. "Then we'll keep it up for six or seven hours until every last bullet has been fired."

The lieutenant saluted his superior officer and made his way back to his platoon, leaving behind a wake of munitions cartridges and smoldering ash.

Nearly a day and a half had passed since the four companions left the bridges behind. They had ridden their lizards through the maze of tunnels below the Park, and they could feel the Tree's presence all around them, smothering and oppressing them as if it knew they were coming. With minimal rest and thankfully few minor complications on the way, they had navigated the length of the prison and had each reached the other end in one piece.

In front of them stood a large triangular door with strange sigils running around its edges. When they approached the portal, the markings glowed red, and the air thickened around them, preventing them from getting any closer.

Kestrel turned to Kase. "Try the key," she

Sídhe

suggested.

The boy obliged and withdrew the key from his pocket, holding it in front of him. As he approached, the markings turned green and allowed him through so he could insert the key into the lock. The lock clicked open and, on silent hinges, drew back into the wall.

A thin shaft of sunlight greeted them, illuminating a stairwell that led up to the forest above. After they let their eyes adjust to the light, they climbed the stairs and exited through a rocky outcropping into the heart of the Sídhe kingdom. They were surrounded by the ancient, gnarled trees of Myrr Wood and immediately felt that they were sorely unwelcome.

Just then a black raven landed on a low branch above Kestrel's head and stared at her with brilliant blue eyes. It took off again, landed in a tree about twenty yards ahead of them, and waited for them to approach. For the next hour they picked their way through the woods like this, following the bird's lead and allowing it to guide them into what they hoped wasn't a trap.

For a while all was well within the forest. The

trees creaked and groaned in the wind, as would be expected, and they could hear and sense the wildlife around them, but nothing came forth to stop or harm them. Though their progress wasn't slowed, they still couldn't shake the feeling that the trees were watching them with invisible eyes.

Suddenly the forest went quiet—completely silent—and a chill ran down everyone's spine. The black raven then dove at Kestrel, smacking her in the arm and landing on a rock at her feet. It stared into the woods behind her and cawed. The elf girl slowly turned her head to look and suddenly went cold. The raven took off and flew back in the direction it was leading them, but much, much faster this time.

The elf clamped down on her fear and kicked up her heels. "*Run!* Follow that bird, and don't look back…just *RUN!*"

The forest went wild. Overwhelming sensations of hatred, fear, and torment surrounded them, and terror filled them. The air crackled with unseen electrical energy, the wind howled through the trunks, and the leaves dropped and blanketed the ground. The trees stirred to life and became a hungry maelstrom of destruction behind the travelers. The wind picked up the soil and churned it into hundreds of small tornadoes that ripped across the ground. With a horrible cracking sound, the trees uprooted and lifted away from the earth beneath them, breaking and distorting to form a solid green-and-brown wave that threatened to overtake them and smash them into the dirt if they slowed.

The little company ran as fast as they could. They could hear and feel the forest chasing after them, but they were too terrified to turn and look back. They were the equivalent of twigs in a hurricane. There was no way to fight; if they stopped, the forest would consume them.

Commander Crashblade checked the level on his plasma thrower and knew he had only about an hour left before it would run dry. Ash covered everything, as far as the eye could see. It rained from the sky, obliterating everything below it from view. He shot blindly now, rocking his weapon back and forth in a wave of destruction; but for every pass he made, another growth of the roots would spring forth. By sheer firepower they were holding the storm at bay, but he could already hear the weapons fire diminishing. Everyone was running critically low on ammunition.

They let Kase lead, and the boy ran as fast as his legs would carry him. Murdox and the elves pushed him from behind, but he had long since passed total exhaustion and was moving forward by way of sheer terror. Fear could only push a person so far, though, and he realized that if he didn't stop soon he would collapse, and it would really be over.

The boy dropped to his knees and fell forward in the dirt, totally spent. Fox grabbed him by the belt and tossed him over his shoulder, carrying him until they reached the edge of the woods and then stumbled into a clearing. As they crossed the threshold of the trees, the woods went quiet behind them…and they dared turn around.

Just as Kestrel had witnessed before, the wave had disappeared. The gnarled trunks and the impossibly green canopy were exactly where they should be. The forest stood as it had for generations. The eyes of the trees were still on them, but there was no evidence that anything out of the ordinary had happened at all.

Ahead of them in the distance and covering the horizon was the enormous trunk of the Tree. It stretched into the sky, ripping a hole in the ceiling of the thirteenth level and twisting and distorting the quantum dimensional physics that held the Park together. Fortunately the magic hadn't been completely compromised and was holding for the moment.

Kase had almost caught his breath when he looked up at the ceiling as it warped and swirled around the Tree's trunk.

"I'll bet this is what it looks like from the inside of my backpack when I pull something out," he said in a hushed voice.

Murdox sat back on his haunches and panted from exertion. "Great! If we don't get killed by the forest first, our molecules will probably explode and scatter into a million pieces when the quantum field fails and we get thrown back into real space."

The remains of the once-proud Faerie City

stood before them. What had been a beautiful metropolis intertwined within the ancient trees of Myrr Wood was now a twisted hulk of shattered buildings and homes. It had been utterly consumed by the Tree. All that remained of the Sídhe capitol was the Queen's castle, standing as a last vestige of the city's existence. Soon the bulk of the Tree would reach it, crushing the stone into sand and obliterating it as well.

Fox took a few steps into the clearing when the forest behind them rumbled again and they could see movement in the trees. From out of the woods came a small battalion of the Queen's army, but he knew her full force wasn't too far behind.

Fox grabbed Kestrel by the arm. "You're the best shot I've ever seen with that bow. Can you hit the Tree from here?"

For an instant Kestrel gauged the distance. "The Tree is as big as a mountain, so of course I could hit it—heck, a dog could—but the arrow wouldn't have nearly enough velocity to break through the bark. I need to get close…really close."

Fox watched as three small swifts shot

overhead, each with a faerie rider on its saddled back. "I've got an idea, but you'll need to hop a ride."

The birds turned in the air and dove down at the little company, and Fox yelled to the group. "*Down…!* Everyone *down now*!"

As a group, they hit the dirt just as the swifts shot overhead, but Fox sprang up from the ground and into the air as the bird passed him. With timing and skill that only a Sentinel could possess, he grabbed one of the faerie riders and wrenched him backwards in his saddle, then jumped aboard, himself.

The swifts were like miniature fighter jets; they were bullets in the sky and masters of aerial acrobatics, but to achieve that kind of skill they had to be small. They could carry only one rider and no extra cargo. Between the force of Fox crashing into it, as well as the Sentinel's extra weight, the bird dropped from the sky and skidded unceremoniously across the ground.

Fox wrenched the unconscious rider from the bird's back and yelled to Kestrel, who was already picking off the first of the ground troops with her bow. "Here you go! Now get to that Tree and finish this."

Kestrel leapt into the saddle as the Sentinel slid off and then grabbed him by the shoulder. "What about you three?"

"Just do it...and hurry! We can hold them off for a few minutes," said Fox as he pulled his bow from his shoulder.

Kestrel nodded and pulled back on the bird's reins, kicking it in the flanks and urging it back into the sky. Fox and his two companions took cover below a low hillock, just beyond the treeline.

Fox looked over at the young IEA agent and was about to give him some instructions when he realized he didn't need any. The boy wasn't much of a shot, but he had his weapon in hand and was doing a pretty fair job of keeping the enemy busy.

Murdox nudged Kase in the leg. "Behind the tree, over there to the right. Get him!"

Kase nodded and pointed his Berrington Model 13 electrostatic energy blaster at the hobgoblin behind the tree and missed.

"I really need more practice at the range with this."

Murdox groaned. "Yes, you do!"

The second shot hit the tree, but the third shot did the trick and engulfed the creature in crackling electricity as it fell to the ground, out cold.

Fox was leveling gnolls and hobgoblins—anything that moved in the trees found one of his arrows heading toward it. For a few moments they were able to hold off the first wave of attackers, but he could already sense that another was on the way. Unfortunately he was just about out of arrows.

-Chapter Eighteen-
The Tree

Kestrel was having her own troubles with the other two swifts. She made a run for the Tree, but the faerie troops who were still on wing cut her off before she made it halfway. They forced the young elf to turn back in the direction of the forest and were accelerating on her. She hit the edge of the woods and turned hard into the trees, trying to get a clear shot across the field and back to the Great Tree. They were good, staying right on her tail, so close that she couldn't lose them. Deftly she cut left and right, up and down through the trunks as they tried to force her from the air.

The elf scout was a seasoned pilot and good at flying under the canopy, but the swift's agility was truly astonishing. Kestrel could stay ahead of the other riders, but doing so forced her into attempting maneuvers that she hadn't believed possible before. This strategy often found her pummeled by the concussive g-forces of the maneuvers, and it took everything she had just to keep from blacking out.

Fox ran out of arrows as the second wave emerged from the woods. He pulled out his sword and raced to the trees, attempting to stay clear of Kase's blaster shots in the process.

The young Sentinel was devastating. He whirled and twirled in a deadly dance that defeated enemies as fast as they could approach. He used the chaos of the scene to his advantage, forcing his attackers to strike wildly in the air, finding one another even more often than a defensive blow from him. His sword blended smoothly from one strike to the next as he parried back with two, three, and sometimes four defenders at one time.

Murdox jumped into the fray when two hunting dogs tried to flank Kase. Pushing off from his powerful hind legs, the wolf-dog leapt into the air and landed on top of one of the attacking canines, bringing it to the ground hard. He charged at the other dog just as it reached the boy, clawing and snapping at the beast with his powerful jaws and trying to provide Kase with a clear shot.

Murdox took a paw to the face and was knocked back into the side of the hill, giving the hunting dog clear access to the young agent. Kase saw the dog coming and rolled out of its way as the beast lunged for him. The young agent followed through on his roll and sprang up at the last second, spinning around on his heel. The dog turned to find the boy again but found only the muzzle of the blaster in his face.

Kestrel circled around the fight and saw that her little company was holding off the attacking horde, but the entire army of the Faerie Nation was about to enter the fray, and at any moment her friends would be overrun. The two other swifts darted in front of her, cutting so close that she could feel their feathers as they passed.

The elf girl tried a daring maneuver. She found an opening in the canopy and spurred her bird to fly straight up into the air, skimming inches away from the lichen-covered bark of the tree, escaping from the forest, and disappearing into the sky. She hit the apex of her climb and rolled the bird onto its back, corkscrewing in the air until she was upright and pointing in the direction of the Tree. The two other swifts followed behind, but Kestrel was nearly at the Tree by the time they had caught up.

She tried to land, but they wouldn't let her get near the ground. Again she pulled the bird skyward, shooting back up into the air and almost vanishing from sight. The two faerie riders caught up with her, and she spun her bird over backwards, dropping from the sky and falling in a death-defying spiral.

She pulled out of the dive at the last possible second, skimming the bird inches above the ground and trying to slow it as much as she could. Just as her pursuers had caught up with her once more, she jumped from the saddle and hit the ground hard, tumbling and rolling head over heels in the dirt.

The roots of the Tree had made it to within

inches of the ground. The city forces had run out of ammunition; there was nothing left to do. A long brown tendril inched its way closer to the ground, and Commander Crashblade pointed his weapon at it and pulled the trigger…but nothing happened. The plasma had been depleted, and the weapon was useless.

Enob tried to destroy the root with his magic, but he collapsed to the ground, completely wrung out. He had nothing left to give, and physical exhaustion finally bested him.

Crashblade grabbed the roots with his bare hands, pulling and tearing them out as fast as he could, but when one broke away, another took its place. Time after time he ripped away the roots with bloody hands, dropping to his knees to catch them before they could hit the soil….

Kase watched as Fox disappeared into the woods. He couldn't see what was happening but could hear the sounds of steel on steel and the final groans of the Sentinel's opponents as they fell to his blade. Kase started shooting his blaster at whatever came out of the woods and, for a moment, thought they might be gaining the upper hand, when suddenly all went silent. He no longer heard the sounds of battle, nor did any more creatures emerge from the woods. The boy was just about to get up from behind the hillock where he had taken cover when he saw Fox crash out of the woods, running at full speed.

Fox surged forward, diving between two goblins and rolling over his shoulder. When he had passed them, he leapt to his feet and twisted around, striking out with his sword in a huge arc and defeating two more of the foul beasts. He turned to confront the next attacker, but they had all disappeared.

He whirled around and around, looking for more foes, but none could be found. That was when he heard the commotion from deep within the trees. The noise got louder and louder, and he realized what he was hearing. The young Sentinel turned on his heels and ran, sprinting as quickly as possible away from the forest and toward Kase and Murdox. Fox bounced off a tree with his shoulder as he broke through the tree line, but he ignored the pain and called out to the two agents.

"Run...! RUN...! Head to the Tree now!"

The Sentinel leaped over the knoll in two bounds, catching up with Kase as the boy dashed across the field as fast as he could.

"What? What is it?" asked Kase hoarsely.

Fox gestured behind him but didn't stop.

Kase looked back for a second and immediately picked up the pace, even pulling slightly ahead of Fox in the process. Murdox was already ahead of them both.

Emerging from the forest for as far as the eye could see was the army of the Faerie Queen in its entirety. Thousands of creatures marched out of the trees. It was a horrifying site, and to be one of three lone soldiers set against a horde of monsters, all set to destroy you, was a disconcerting feeling.

Kase ran faster.

Kestrel tried to stand, but she had broken an ankle in the fall. She watched as the two swifts quickly approached, and knew she wouldn't be able to defend herself against the fast-moving birds. She pulled her sword from its sheath and crouched in the dirt, trying to protect herself from the attack.

Out of nowhere the black raven swooped in directly between the swifts and the elf scout. Before it even hit the ground, its spine rippled and its feathers fell away from its body. Its outline blurred and contorted, growing in size and shape until it finally resolved into an enormous faerie hound. The creature must have weighed more than three hundred pounds. It resembled a large greyhound with a silvery coat and a crest of long quills that ran down its spine. It turned to Kestrel and watched the elf with neon blue eyes, as if deciding what to do.

In a streak of white and brown, the swifts banked as one and headed right at the elf scout. Before they could reach her, the Queen's faerie hound bounded into the air right in front of them. They tried to swerve and get out of the way, but with incredible speed the faerie hound yanked them both from the sky with a single swipe of his massive paw.

Kestrel removed the black arrow from her quiver, its blade reflecting the light and flaring in the afternoon sun. She nocked the arrow and drew back her bow, aiming it directly at the Great Tree.

She released the string and the bolt sailed through the air striking the Tree, sinking deep into the bark till only the tail feathers were visible. For an instant nothing happened, and then a small gray ring began to radiate outward from the arrow, blackening everything in its passing. Black splotches swelled along the grain of the Tree, and the bark began falling away in huge chunks, hitting the ground and breaking apart.

The root touched the ground directly in front of Commander Devin Crashblade, and a faint yellow glow ignited at the point where it came in contact with the soil. The light grew in intensity and began to rise upward along its length but then suddenly went out. In front of his eyes, the root turned gray, then black, and finally disintegrated into a pile of dust.

The three companions ran toward the Tree, trying to escape from the army of the Queen. Wave after wave of arrows and spears hit the ground behind them, but they were losing ground, and with every step the danger got closer and closer to their heels.

Fox was just about to grab Kase to quicken their pace, but there was suddenly no need. The entire Tree turned black against the blue of the sky—a huge, ominous shape that stretched outward—then a great wind took it, and it blew away in a cloud of soot. The sky rained ash, blanketing the ground in every direction for as far as they could see, and by the time they reached Kestrel, they were all covered in the black grime.

The army stopped in their tracks, dazed and confused. The Queen's magic that had held them in its sway fell aside with the wind.

Some wandered the field, witless, and others fled back to the dark pits they called home. A few of the races banded together to wage war on their mutual sworn enemies, and small skirmishes broke out amidst the ash...but most fled from the field and quietly disappeared back into the trees.

The Faerie Queen emerged from the ash still

clutching the staff. She smiled faintly at the small company and then collapsed to the ground.

The faerie hound ambled up to its Queen and nudged her with its cold nose. She stirred at its touch but didn't wake. The great hound grabbed the staff between its teeth and took it over to Kestrel, dropping it at her feet. The creature looked up at each of them and smiled in a way that only a dog can. It then turned from them and lay down to guard its Queen, resting its head on it paws.

-Epilogue-

It had been more than two weeks since the Faerie Queen's assault had been defeated and the Tree had been destroyed. Once more Fox found himself on wing over the southern ocean, flying through the darkness of the pre-dawn hours. The young Sentinel was riding upon his falcon, Stormwise, and was getting a bit saddle sore but still happy to be on the final leg of a tiring adventure. He was accompanied on this trip by Kestrel, who was riding on the back of her great horned owl, sound asleep and apparently quite content.

After the Tree had fallen, the little company had made their way back into Myrr Wood to escape any fae folk that might have some difficult questions to ask that they didn't really want to answer. Their progress was slow because of Kestrel's broken ankle, but they managed to find a safe place, far enough away from the crushed city that trouble didn't find them.

During their respite the forest continued to watch them in a strange, sentient way, but this time the overall mood wasn't hostile, but rather comfortingly serene. They needn't have worried about retribution from the Sídhe, either; they were not a hostile or vengeful race. The Queen herself was an honorable and kind woman, but the genetics of her ancient lineage had forced her to do what she did. Just as she held her army in thrall, the staff held her, and she could not control its overwhelming power. When the Tree had collapsed, the magic that held the Queen and her army in its sway faded, and they were all freed from its grip.

The Tree would have changed the future. The Faerie race would have returned to power, and the world would have broken out in a great war. Countless lives would have been lost in a supremacy struggle that could only be won by the Tree itself. No one wanted this, especially the Sídhe. For generations the fae folk had no desire to conquer or to wield this kind of power. They were content in the Park, hidden from the world and at peace with their surroundings. In the distant future might come a time when they would again seek to rule…but that time was not now. They had a city to rebuild and apologies to make for the atrocities that their kind had committed while under control of the staff's magic. Some would understand, but many would not—and they had a long road to travel before trust could be gained again.

The Queen herself would never be the same. The staff's magic had given her near-omnipotence within the Park. While in the grip of the enchantment, she could hear the mental chatter of every creature under her control. Their voices and thoughts threatened to drive her mad, nearly destroying her. Utilizing an inner strength she hadn't known she possessed, she had managed to lock away a little bit of her true self back in the far reaches of her mind. With this tiny bit of sanity, she had instructed her faerie hound to seek out those who might rectify this situation. In its usual unwavering devotion, the Queen's close companion and guardian had fulfilled its mission and helped to make things right.

Once Kestrel was better fit to travel, the little company had taken to the road again and returned to her village in the trees. They had time on their side now, and the pace was much more leisurely. They arrived only to learn that the magic that controlled the portal between the Park and the rest of Cloudview was still unstable, and they would not yet be able to exit that level safely.

The sylvan elves opened their homes to Kestrel's traveling companions and invited them to stay as long as needed. It was a wonderful little vacation for the group, and they managed to heal their battle wounds and wind back down to a more normal life…or at least a more normal pace. It also gave Fox and Kestrel some leisure time to become even better acquainted, and Fox was able to share a number of Sentinel training techniques with the scout, as well, which was very gratifying to her.

When the Park gate was working once again, Kase and Murdox headed back to their offices at the IEA to help with Cloudview's recovery. They weren't foolish enough to hope that the metropolis had been spared damage from the Tree, but neither were they prepared for what they found. From the thirtieth level down, the place they called home was utterly devastated. That Cloudview was still standing could only be called a miracle of true engineering genius…and a lot of powerful magic. Rebuilding would take years, but it would be done, and the metropolis would eventually be better than it was before.

The sun rose over the vast expanse of ocean, driving away the darkness before the two elves. Not long after the exquisite dawn, Fox spotted his destination, and they circled their birds around the small atoll known as Halfway Island. When all was deemed clear, the young elves pointed their birds to a long plateau and brought the magnificent creatures in for a landing near a freshwater pool.

They dismounted and stretched their sore, weary muscles. Then Fox removed a small pouch from his flight bag and pulled open the draw string. From the pouch he withdrew a small lump of brown clay, which he rolled between his palms until it was round.

Kestrel untied a long cloth wrapping from the back of her rig and laid it on the ground next to her owl.

She unfurled the material and removed the staff, allowing her fingers to run over its smooth wood grain. Fox watched her for a moment and nodded that it was time, and the elf scout rolled the staff back into the material's folds.

The young Sentinel placed the clay ball on the ground in front of him and traced a mystic sigil into the soft material. He whispered a password into the clay and let the magic do the rest.

The rocky ground directly under the clay shuddered and cracked, breaking apart until it revealed a long rectangular cavity, similar to a grave. In the hole was a bulky canvas parcel about the size of a large book. Kestrel gazed at the bundle for a moment, wondering what it held, but Fox didn't utter a word.

The young Sentinel picked up the staff, still wrapped in its protective cloth, and tossed it in alongside the other object, seemingly without a second thought. Then he stepped back from the magical opening and once more whispered under his breath the secret password. The ground shuddered, and the rock in front of Fox knitted itself back together, leaving behind only the small ball of clay.

"If this keeps up," he said, "it's going to get awfully crowded in there."

He picked up the clay and squeezed it in his palm until it oozed between his fingers. Then quite unceremoniously he dumped the clay back into its bag and tossed that into his flight pack.

Kestrel smiled. "Maybe you won't have to secure anything else in there for a while," she suggested hopefully.

Fox looked dubious. "The way things seem to go, I'm afraid that's not too likely," he replied, then added, "but maybe I won't have to go it alone next time around, either. That sure helped on this operation!"

Kestrel grinned proudly until her dimples showed, and Fox couldn't help but grin back. Despite his training and discipline, the Sentinel felt his face begin to flush before he could regain control over it. He turned to cinch down his gear again and stroked Stormwise's wing.

The young elves rested, watered and fed the birds, and shared a snack before climbing into their saddles again. Soon they were back on wing, with the island in the distance far behind them.

www.ingramcontent.com/pod-product-compliance
Lightning Source LLC
LaVergne TN
LVHW091531060526
838200LV00036B/561